Praise for
Crooked Roads: Crime Stories

"With fists pounding against cliché and convention, Alec Cizak creates prose that is bold...and bloody."

—David Cranmer,
editor of *Beat to a Pulp*

Praise for Alec Cizak's Other Works

"With *Down on the Street*, Alec Cizak writes the best dirtbag noir since Jed Ayres' *Peckerwood*. There are delights in the darkness and you'll hate yourself for laughing out loud, but it's inevitable. Not an easy read for the gender studies set, but who cares what they're reading anyway? You won't want it to end."

—Eryk Pruitt, author of
What We Reckon

"*Down on the Street* reminds me of the darker side of Bukowski. Cizak's a writer who cares about language, about getting it right, about giving the reader something of worth. The characters are despicable. You wouldn't want them in the same room with your children. But you'll care about them. Even identify with their plight. And then you'll want to reconsider your own morals and the luxuries that allowed you to have them."

—Grant Jerkins, author of
Abnormal Man

D1598123

CROOKED ROADS

ROADS

Crime Stories

Other Titles by Alec Cizak

Between Juarez and El Paso
Manifesto Destination
Down on the Street

ALEC CIZAK

CROOKED ROADS

crime Stories

ALL
DUE
RESPECT

All Due Respect
An imprint of Down & Out Books
3959 Van Dyke Rd, Ste. 265
Lutz, FL 33558
www.DownAndOutBooks.com

Edited by Rob Pierce and Chris Rhatigan
Cover design by Eric Beetner

ISBN: 1-946502-97-9
ISBN-13: 978-1-946502-97-1

CONTENTS

*For Mrs. Moore, my sixth grade teacher.
She taught me that imagination and
creativity have value in this world.*

THE SPACE BETWEEN

She wears a nametag—Susan. You want her to be more. To see the gray smudges on the bottom of your pants legs, to put a hand on your shoulder and say, "That snow bank sure *seemed* solid." She should notice the gash across your left, index knuckle. Wince at how the wound has turned yellow and brown. "Sometimes we forget to aim the knife away from our bodies," she should say. Beyond that, she should offer empathy over the alimony you can't pay, the money you owe the IRS, the foreclosure. "An apartment might be more manageable, don't you think?" The angle her head rests on her shoulders, the light bouncing off her eyes, the smile she greeted you with when the bell over the front door went "ding," these things dissolve layers of hatred gathering mold since your wife insinuated you're a "mama's boy." They cancel the sneers in college, the snubs from attractive sorority girls, the signs stuck to your back in high school (*Kick Me!*). Your father's fist, once a ton, now evaporates with a chuckle from you as Susan drops a cliché on the counter—"Cold enough for you?" You don't hear the formality of the situation. You don't

1

realize this relationship is over the moment you pay and walk out the door.

The creak of your car door slices into your ears and carves canyons in your bones. Did you think the girl at the Kwik Trip would look at you twice? As you turn the ignition and wait for the heater to fire up, watching the fog of your breath splatter against the windshield and shrink, over and over again, you listen to the voice of reason on the radio (*This country ain't what it used to be!*) and remember how you will spend the night in a motel with nothing but a television, mini bottles of shampoo, small towels, and a Gideon's Bible that can do nothing to correct mistakes you've made your entire life. Mistakes other people tricked you into making—

Your mother, dressing you in clothes from Second Time Around.

Your father, refusing to look at you after you said you had no interest in baseball.

Junior high girlfriends, lovers, and the wife, calling you one form of inadequate or another.

Would Susan be any different? She doesn't care about you, chump. Look at her now—can't you hear the smacking of her bubblegum? She's in uniform, on the clock, and yet she has her cellphone pasted to her ear. Remember the way she spoke to you, thinking you wouldn't catch the disregard her cliché revealed?

The car's warm.

There's a tire iron in the trunk.

Haven't you reached that point where you could just *drive*?

"The Space Between" first appeared in *Shotgun Honey*.

COLUMBUS DAY

6:19 p.m.

Kristos jammed the end of the shotgun into Hector's mouth and pulled the trigger. Bump had never seen somebody get killed. Not actually. He hadn't been hanging out with Kristos for too long. His throat went dry when Kristos first handed him the Benelli and said, "You do it."

Bump said, "Jeez, let's just take his stuff."

"You some kind of bitch?" Kristos said.

Hector reached for a dirty steak knife that had fallen on the floor. Carpet and cat hair stuck to what looked like dried spaghetti sauce. So Kristos took the gun back and shot him. Afterwards, he said, "I had no choice."

Bump said, "Oh yeah, I know. Sure, sure. I know."

They finished the rails on the coffee table, the ones without blood in them. Then they tore the house apart. Flipped couches and chairs. Knocked the fridge over, pulled drawers in the kitchen, dumped plastic spoons and knives all over the floor. Kristos said it needed to look like an army had plowed through the joint.

5

They returned to the yuppie's SUV with a freezer bag of meth and ninety-two bucks.

4:12 p.m.

They left Sophia to watch after the yuppie's wife. Drove the yuppie's car, a black Escalade. Bump couldn't breathe. Had to be eighty degrees outside. He said, "Good grief, what happened to autumn?" He tugged at his ski mask.

Kristos smacked him. "You stupid?"

The yuppie, hands tied behind him, mumbled through the sock stuffed in his mouth. Something like, "I won't tell anybody." He'd been saying the same thing since they busted into his house. His wife, right along with him, like a night club act—

Him: "We won't squeal, honest."

Her: "Yeah, honest, we won't."

They stopped at an ATM in Owatonna. Kristos held the barrel of the shotgun to the yuppie's temple. Bump removed the gag and untied the rope around his hands.

"First thing," Kristos said to the yuppie, "let me see your account balances. All of them, fucker."

The yuppie nodded. He'd given no resistance since his awful afternoon began. And it must have been awful. Bump couldn't imagine being on the other side of the situation.

"Remember," said Kristos, "you do anything stupid, any goddamn thing at all, and we'll cut you down right here, go back to your house, rape your fucking wife, and kill her, too."

"Yes sir," the yuppie said.

He stepped out, walked to the ATM, shoved his card in, and brought back a slip of paper. Bump couldn't believe the numbers. The guy might as well have been sitting on gold.

"You know," the yuppie said, "I can't draw more than three hundred from the same ATM."

"That's fine," Kristos said. "We can hit every machine between here and Mankato. We've got all day."

They took the last of the yuppie's money in Waseca. The total haul: nearly fifteen-hundred.

Bump said, "What do you do for a living?"

"I'm a claims adjustor at Farmers."

"Well then," Kristos said, "looks like we're just robbing a fancier breed of thief."

"Maybe so," the yuppie said.

Bump wanted to ask him why he would agree so quickly to an insult, but decided not to.

"Hector is sitting on a stash," Kristos said. "We do this proper, things'll work out better than we ever imagined."

3:49 p.m.

Kristos said they were just going to get some crank and head back to his place to chill and watch the Vikings on Monday Night Football. He said folks were using a new house in the Fairland development to cook. Said they'd bust in, take whatever they'd made, and book right back to New Ulm.

Sophia said, "Cool."

Bump said, "Jeez, why don't we just buy some from them?"

Kristos glared at him in the rearview. "Don't be a little faggot, now."

They pulled into the development. Most of the houses were still under construction. Bulldozers sat on the dirt where grass would eventually be installed. Three pickup trucks lined the roads. Nobody working. Maybe because of the holiday. At the farthest end of the first cul-de-sac, a black SUV occupied the driveway of a finished house.

"Must be it," Kristos said. He parked and popped the trunk.

They walked around to the back of the car. Kristos handed out ski masks and loaded the shotgun. He put extra shells in the breast pocket of his flannel and closed the trunk. Bump stood still, stared at the ski mask.

"Gosh, we really doing this?"

Kristos forced the mask over his head. "Get your shit together."

Sophia said ouch as she put on hers, no doubt catching fabric on one of the four hundred piercings on her face. Her left cheek rolled as she chewed a piece of gum. She followed Kristos, snapped her fingers at Bump. "The fuck you waiting for?"

They ducked near the front door. Kristos peered into the picture window on the other side. He scratched his head, crouched down, and snuck back to Bump and Sophia. "They got nice sweaters on," he said. "You know that means they got money."

"Well," Sophia said, "shit."

"Maybe the cook's happening somewhere else," Bump said.

"Don't matter," Kristos said. "We'll rob these motherfuckers and buy some legitimate shit."

They crept to the door. Sophia clapped her hands at Bump. "Get it up," she said.

Kristos beat the door handle with the butt of the gun until the lock gave. He barged in, gun raised. Sophia marched behind him. "Get your asses on the ground," she said.

Bump looked at the flat land surrounding him, just beyond the half-finished houses. If he ran, Kristos would have to make a decision.

Sophia poked her head out the door. "Get your stupid ass in here, boy."

He climbed the steps, wiped his feet on the Welcome mat, and entered the house.

The place looked as though someone had lived there a long time already. Smooth, oval table in the dining room. Beautiful, plush couch in the TV room. And the TV on the wall, holy cow, a small movie screen. A window at the top of the staircase blasted sun into the house as though God had designed the place Himself. Nothing like the trailer Bump stayed in with his mom. Then he saw the yuppies, sprawled on the floor with their hands covering their necks.

"Anybody else here?" said Sophia.

"It's just us," the man said. His voice cracked. "And

now, you." He was crying. So was the woman.

Kristos draped the shotgun over his shoulders. He paraded back and forth between the dining room and the TV room. "This shit looks like paradise."

"Sure does," Bump said. "Sure, sure does."

Sophia flopped onto the couch. She pressed random buttons on a giant remote until the TV channel changed. She found some reality show about rich girls in LA with big butts. "I can die now," she said.

Kristos asked about money.

The man pulled his wallet from his pocket. He showed him the two twenties in it. Kristos took it from him and shuffled through the plastic. "These good for ATMs?"

7:09 p.m.

The yuppie mumbled through his gag. Said something like, "Are you guys okay?"

Kristos said, "The fuck you talking about?"

The man said he heard a gunshot.

"Worry about yourself," Kristos said. He put the Caddie in drive and did the speed limit back to the housing development.

Bump opened the bag of meth, scooped some onto his pinky and snorted it.

"Ain't you had enough already?" Kristos said. "Fucking junkie."

Times like that, Bump wondered why he hung out with him and Sophia. They made constant fun of him, said stuff like, "Is it true you all don't know your sisters from your mamas?" Like they were better than him, like they *hadn't* grown up on a rundown rez outside Bemidji.

"I've never seen this much at once," said Bump. He carved out another hit. Made sure he was so high he couldn't feel a thing.

Kristos snatched the bag from him. "You're going to waste this shit. Fucking junkie."

The yuppie said something like, "Should you guys be driving right now?"

"Fucking white boy," Kristos said. He turned on the radio. NPR. "Faggot shit," he said, and punched the dial until he found a classic rock station.

Bump stared out the window. He stared at the border of the horizon. Hardly seemed that far away. He closed his eyes and imagined himself a giant, stomping across the Minnesota countryside, cracking the Earth with every step.

7:41 p.m.

Bump's heart beat in his chest like a couple of tribal drums. He clawed at the bottom of his mask, wanted to rip it off. Was it possible to be blinded by your own sweat?

Kristos dragged the yuppie from the Caddie. Rushed him across the tiny lawn with his free hand wrapped around his hair. Then he pitched him onto the porch. "Let your wifey know you're home." He kicked the door in and threw him into the TV room.

Bump's toes throbbed inside his shoes. His chewed sneakers looked like they were breathing.

Sophia sat on the couch, vegging to some other reality show. The yuppie's wife leaned to her side, weeping. Half her blonde hair had been braided, like Sophia's. "You boys got good news?" Sophia said.

"Let's go," Kristos said.

"Sweet."

Bump scratched his right arm. He knew there were worms crawling just under his skin. He could hear air-conditioning, why the heck was it so gosh darned hot? He took his mask off and said so.

Everyone stared at him.

"You dumb motherfucker," Kristos said. He peeled his mask over his face, wore it like a snowcap.

Sophia took hers off and dropped it on the floor.

"Guess we got to stay a while." Kristos grabbed the yuppie from the floor and threw him on the couch, next to his wife. "Might as well have fun." He lifted the yuppie's wife's face by her chin. "You like to suck dick?" he said.

"Bullshit," Sophia said. "You put your junk any-where near her, I'll cut it off while you sleep."

They circled each other, like school kids on a play-ground. Kristos stuck his tongue out, flicked it side to side.

Bump said, "They'll be cool." He believed it, too. He transmitted a message to the yuppies, psychically, told them to keep their traps shut.

"Doubt it," Kristos said. "You think your sister, or

mom, or whoever the fuck that bitch is you live with, you think she'd mind if you wet your dick in this rich bitch?"

Bump shook his head. "I don't need that right now," he said.

Kristos leapt at him and twisted the collar of his T-shirt around his fist. "You totally FUBAR'd this mission," he said. "You make it worthwhile for all of us." He let him go and put his arm around Sophia.

The yuppie rolled over, stared at Bump. He spit the sock in his mouth onto the couch. "Don't touch her." Like he assumed Bump could be threatened, knowing damn well he'd never talk like that to Kristos.

Bump wanted to kick him in his face. Before he could say anything, though, Kristos turned the shotgun around and smashed the yuppie's skull until it popped like a watermelon and splashed blood across the couch.

"Jeez," Bump said.

"Cool," Sophia said, chewing her gum faster.

The yuppie's wife slumped off the couch. Red slime covered her blouse. She screamed through her gag and kicked at the nice, glass coffee table.

"You going to fuck this bitch, or what?" Kristos said.

The woman shook her head. "No way," she said.

This made Bump angrier. Every single person in the room, telling him his business. "*Bitch*," he said, "I'm going to do whatever the hell I want to do."

"Well go ahead," Sophia said. She shoved him hard enough to send him over the glass table, onto the woman.

"There it is," said Kristos. "Hit that bitch like she's your mom!"

The woman squirmed. Bump reached for her breasts. He couldn't ignore the goo from her husband's brain, leaking through her blouse. And he knew he wouldn't be able to get hard for all the gold in the world. Nothing sexy about a woman doused in gore. He tried thinking of Kendra, a friendly girl from Mankato who let him put her hand in her panties when they were teenagers. That usually did the trick when he jerked off. Just that memory—the first time he slipped his fingers inside a woman. But even that didn't work.

"I can't do it."

Pointing at the dead yuppie, Kristos said, "Did I kill this one too soon?"

Sophia laughed.

The woman said something like, "Don't listen to them."

Nothing worse than someone assuming you were the same, just so you wouldn't hurt them. "You think you're smart?" Bump said. He stretched his hand out for the gun.

Kristos stepped back. "Oh, *shit*." He gave him the Benelli.

It looked like an antique, like something Bump's great-great-great granddaddy might have used in the Indian Wars. "Sympathize with this," he said. He jammed the barrel into the sock in the woman's mouth and pulled the trigger. The backsplash soaked him.

"*Goddamn*," said Kristos.

"Well," Sophia said, "guess we should head."

Bump said, "I got a better idea."

Kristos grinned, made it seem, for the first time, like he gave a shit about anything he had to say.

"This house belongs to us," said Bump. "Let's call some folks, have a party."

"Columbus Day" first appeared in Dark Corners.

NO HARD FEELINGS

A Quick Word about My Daddy

My daddy always said, never underestimate the stupid other folks is capable of. He accidentally blew his brains out with a pistol one night. Thought it wasn't loaded. Kept sticking it in his mouth and pulling the trigger. Guess a bullet had hid in there or something. Put his skull all over the wall behind the couch in the family room. The couch *I* slept on. Mama said she weren't none surprised. Said Daddy weren't too bright himself. The hell knows? All I remember is sitting on a lawn chair outside the trailer, waiting for folks to clean the mess so I could get some sleep.

Missy Vaughn

Missy Vaughn said we was something. Said so all over Haggard High. Fine by me. I knew she let me cork her to get revenge on her daddy. Now, I ain't calling her daddy one of them uppercase fellows what liked to poke his own daughter. Didn't seem that type to me. But he

17

had a strange sense of humor that could suffocate you. And he never tried to hide his disappointment that his daughter got plowed on the weekends by a resident of Neptune Park.

The Vaughns lived in a house. Like all respectable folks. Third or fourth time I come over to get with Missy, her daddy asked me if I ever had trouble finding their place. Like I might be too stupid to remember where I've been before. Real funny guy. They lived in Ravenswood, this jigsaw puzzle cookie-cutter development near Merrillville. Houses looked like buildings I seen in a Robin Hood movie.

I played along, though. I said to Mr. Vaughn, "Took me a while, sir."

He went into this bit about how that didn't offend him. On and on, he went—"Oh, Dwayne," he said to me, "I'm not the least bit upset about that, not the least." Over and over and over. I could see why his daughter wanted to jab him a little the way daughters always jabbed their daddies—with her choice of boyfriend. If the thought of trailer trash corking her didn't make her daddy break down and cry, she'd go to college and run a few black fellows through her. Eventually, when things like bills and survival became an issue, she'd settle down with the type of man her father had told her to go for from the beginning. You know, *rich*.

But I liked Missy. She kept her area between her legs fresh. I never once got a whiff of what I smelled inside the girls from Neptune Park. And she'd read to me after we smashed. All this fancy stuff she needed to know in order to sound smart if she decided to go to college. Fancy stuff like that Freud fellow. He said everybody did everything they did just to get laid. I didn't need some fruitcake from Europe to point that out, but the way he put it sounded better than any way I could. She also read to me about Marx and Engels. Pretended like she gave a shit about the fact that me and Mama had just enough money to pay rent on our lot. That we used a rusty space heater from the last century to keep the trailer warm in winter. She said someday working class folks would kick the rich right square in their gold-plated beanbags. Fine with me.

Well, we went at it one night in her bedroom, quiet but vicious. She tired out before I did, said, "Finish, already." So I filled her up and rolled over. I caught my breath while she scraped between her legs with tissue. She said, "You know Bill Shipwick, lives across the street?"

"Sure," I said. Bill Shipwick used to be the football coach at Haggard High. Never took the team to state. His wife died in a car wreck a few years back. Semi hopped across the rail on 65 and turned her Buick into an accordion. Only contact I'd ever had with Bill Shipwick was at the drive-in off the exit to Crown Point. I stole Daddy's truck to take this big girl named Tricia to see one of them *Transformer* movies. Had no interest in the show. Just wanted to plow Tricia somewhere our parents couldn't stumble in and laugh at us. So we're waiting in line with a bunch of other cars. Gates ain't opened yet. SUV behind me starts honking. I looked in the rearview like, *Hey, buddy, can't you see nobody's moving?* Well, that yuppie wagon just kept on barking. So I rolled down the window and shouted, "Quit with the fucking horn already!" Next thing I knew, Bill Shipwick marched up, fists clenched. He started hollering, "My *what* horn? My *WHAT* horn?" Once upon a time, that man might have been a contender.

I said, "Why the hell are you honking so damn much?"

He gave me a boo-hoo about how he had his grandkids in the car and they were "just having fun."

I said, "That's disrespectful, honking for no reason."

So he called me a jerk.

I looked at Tricia. She shook her head, like she understood I'd have clobbered that fossil with one pop.

"Old man," I said to Bill Shipwick, "get the hell away from my car."

He nodded, like he'd won a pissing contest or something, and marched back to his fancy SUV. Called me a jerk one last time.

"Yeah," I said to Missy, "I sure do know who Bill Shipwick is."

She finished cleaning my stain from her thighs and told me Bill Shipwick won the Hoosier Millions.

"What?" I had to hear it again.

She said he'd circled the block holding the ticket over his head like a trophy, telling folks how he'd been patiently playing the same numbers for ten years and it finally paid off.

"How much?" I asked.

She said she wasn't sure. "Minimum bucket," she said, "is always a million."

"Good for him," I said. Maybe he'd get the hell out of Lake County and move somewhere nice, where the sky hadn't turned piss yellow and sick gray from the smokestacks in Gary.

Missy laughed. "Don't you get it?"

"Sure," I said. "Some folks are lucky, others aren't."

"*We're* lucky," she said.

"How's that?"

"You're going to take that ticket from him and we're going to escape."

"How the hell am I going to get his ticket?"

Well now, manicured girls like Missy Vaughn understood instinct-wise how to use what they had to persuade any man to do anything they needed. She nuzzled under my chin, kissed all over my chest, rubbed her little titties against me. "Don't you want to run away?" she said. "Don't you want to be with me?" she said. "Don't you want to be rich?"

That last question? No-brainer. She snaked her tongue down my chest, showed me why the first two were just as easy to answer.

Bill Shipwick

I suppose you could call it a generalizing-type of excuse, but I decided Bill Shipwick had enough. He lived in Ravenswood. In a McMansion, goddammit. So his wife died, so what? Life's mostly suffering. You got a house instead of a trailer, you shouldn't do much by way of complaining. That's what I told myself the night I put on a black T-shirt and jeans and snuck through the shadows of Haggard. Tougher to do in Ravenswood because all the streetlights worked.

I almost bashed the old man's front door down. Then I seen he had stickers for Yale Security on his windows. Sometimes that shit meant something, most-wise it didn't. Just a show, to scare off folks like me. I ducked around the back, found a stick about half as heavy as a baseball bat and threw it against a door that looked like it led to Bill Shipwick's kitchen. Nothing happened. No alarms, no lights came on. No rent-a-cops itching to hand me off to the real police.

A few smacks near the latch on a window and I jarred the lock loose and slid it open. Took a struggle, but I managed to wiggle my way in before tumbling to the floor. Knocked my skull on a small, round table. In the dark, I could make out a calendar on the wall from 2012. Maybe that's when Bill Shipwick's old lady died. I didn't remember. I sifted through pieces of paper on top of a cabinet. Didn't see nothing that looked like a lottery ticket. I moved into the kitchen, found a lot of bingo cards. Not sure what the hell Bill Shipwick had them for.

Down the hallway I crept, trying to figure what that old man did with the damn ticket. I pushed a door open to a room filled with bookshelves. Hard to believe Bill Shipwick read anything. Missy would have liked it, though. I wondered if I should take some, you know, for when we hit the road with all that money.

A shadow crossed a light on the second floor. The steps creaked awful rough. Then I saw Bill Shipwick, crouched close to the wall with a shotgun.

"You got about three seconds," he said. I guess a man's proud enough, he don't stop looking for a fight until they dress him up in pine.

"Mr. Shipwick," I said. I held my hands high, hoping he wouldn't get anxious and pop a shell. "I'm just here for the lottery ticket." I made my way out of the library, toward the bottom of the stairs.

He said, "You fixed on going to jail?"

I could smell that old person stink—you know, like Band-Aids or something. "Mr. Shipwick," I said, "I'm not here to cause no trouble. I just want that ticket so me and my girl can have a nice life someplace else." I grabbed the barrel of the shotgun before he responded and slammed the butt into his face. He flew against the wall, blood spilling from his nose.

"I'm a head upstairs," I said. "You stay put." I took the gun with me.

The first two rooms on the second floor were empty. I kind of got angry, thinking about all us folks in Neptune Park, crammed in these tiny aluminum cans while folks in Ravenswood had so much space they didn't even need half of it. I found the old man's bedroom. You'd have thought he lived in a black and white sitcom. Two single beds, separated by a nightstand. Bill Shipwick's keys and wallet were on it. Sure enough, I looked in the wallet and found it—a Hoosier Millions ticket. Had to be the one. I stuffed it in my pocket and tossed the shotgun on one of the beds.

The bannister groaned as Bill Shipwick pulled himself onto the second floor landing. He couldn't breathe too regular, but he felt like wasting air anyway—"Listen here," he said, "I'm going to do what your father obviously failed to do."

"You don't know nothing about my daddy," I said. I tried to walk around him, but he grabbed me, yanked on my shirtsleeve. I pulled away hard enough to send him tumbling right back down the stairs. I followed him, normal-wise, of course, and stepped over him to get to the front door. He didn't move. He'd probably learned his lesson.

I considered cashing the ticket myself. I turned it over and read the instructions. It said it would have to be mailed in. So I went to Missy's, climbed the gutter near her window.

"You got it?" she said.

"Sure, baby." I gave it to her.

"This is it?" she said.

"Says Hoosier Millions, don't it?"

"Crap," she said. "Mr. Shipwick's an idiot." She held the ticket in my face.

"What?"

"Look, dummy," she said. "Mr. Shipwick's been saying he played the same numbers for ten years." She pointed to the date at the bottom. "He's been playing the same *ticket*."

"That's funny," I said. I guessed we wouldn't be going nowhere after all. "You got some grape juice or something?" My throat had gone dry. Couldn't have told you why if I had known myself.

One Last Word about My Daddy

There's been a lot said about me in the newspapers. For whatever reason, they like comparing me to my daddy. I suppose that's okay. I loved him, even when he beat me for being dumb. Like that time he told me to get rid of the leaves on the gravel by our trailer. I gathered them together and dumped lighter fluid on them. I guess one of the flames jumped to a tire on the trailer. Melted the rubber. My daddy made me put the fire out with my winter coat. Promised I'd be thinking about what I did come December and January, when I'd be walking to school with nothing but a sweatshirt and jeans. He wasn't lying. That winter got cold as hell.

"No Hard Feelings" first appeared in *Beat to a Pulp*.

AMERICAN CHIVALRY

It was Wednesday. January rains were in full force. The sidewalks were minefields of puddles and people wore their ugliest faces. None of that would have mattered to Rex Burris had he not lived by the mercy of strangers. For whatever reason, when the sky opened and showered the buildings and soaked the concrete, the pockets of those capable of charity dried up. Rex resorted to less than commendable means of getting what he needed. The last time he was threatened with an empty take, he rolled an anorexic actress wanna-be on the 4 bus. Today, he would haunt the 20 bus on Wilshire, going from downtown to Westwood. Santa Monica, if necessary.

It had taken him the entire morning to collect the buck twenty-five needed to board the 20. The suits and ties and fancy office skirts waddled past with glassy stares. Not a single, "Sorry, I have nothing," followed by a half-hearted pat-down of the pockets. The men stalked on with their backs stiff and the women raised their snouts as though that might lift them up and over the offending man in the doorway asking for spare change. Rex averaged twenty-five cents an hour and feared he might miss the afternoon bus. That would be disastrous. The 20 was fruitful only when Korean wives rolled out of bed, dolled themselves up, and headed west to spend their husbands' money at The Grove. Koreans carried cash. Always.

As the clock tower at the Catholic church on Kingsley and Wilshire struck noon, people flooded out of the offices to eat lunch. Rex collected the final fifty cents in a twenty-minute span.

He hustled to the depot at the corner of Wilshire and Vermont. Mexican and Korean schoolchildren protested when they got a whiff of him. He smiled and nodded, hoping he'd lodge a nugget of guilt in their consciences. The only people that ever seemed to work on, however, were goofy white kids who made the mistake of leaving Iowa to come to LA to make movies.

The bus arrived and made a show of braking before it hissed like a dragon and the doors opened. As Rex climbed on board, he got the usual looks of distress from the proper passengers. First they smelled him, then they saw him. After an unconsciously prompted look of horror, some lowered their faces in shame. The Mexicans and Latinos cupped their hands over their noses.

He chose the seat closest to the back door. Nobody else wanted it because someone had slashed it open and pulled out the Styrofoam stuffing in a clump resembling a heap of mashed potatoes. Graffiti, fashioned with permanent blue and black markers, decorated the cushion on the back of the bench. One messenger, no doubt a Crip, had written *Fucc Slobs*. Someone else, unaffiliated, crossed out the original greeting and scribbled *Western Avenue Hoodsta' Killa'* over it. Rex stuffed as much of the Styrofoam back into the seat as he could and sat with his left leg lifted higher than his right. His location allowed him to size up everyone who got on. He hoped a Korean woman boarded sometime before they reached La Brea. If that didn't happen, he would have to wait for a white girl. Either scenario involved following the woman when she got off, grabbing her at the perfect moment, snatching her purse, and running. He prayed for a Korean woman. They always had enough cash on them to buy two or three fifths of whiskey. A single bottle would get him through the night. He could settle down and sleep anywhere, even in the rain.

At Hobart, a Korean woman with sparkling red and silver manicured nails, no older than twenty-eight or twenty-nine, stepped onto the bus. She opened her purse, maybe Marc Jacobs or Prada, Rex could never tell the difference, with her thin fingers and pulled out a billfold. Flipping through the money inside, she produced exact change and paid her fare. She sat in the front, on a seat reserved for senior citizens and expecting mothers. She wore thigh-high leather boots and a plaid skirt. Her white, button-down shirt was opened wide enough to let anyone interested see that her husband had bought her perfect, balloon-sized breasts. Her eyes and face were shaded to make her look like a magazine model. Had she not been sent to America with children to look after, she could very well have gone to Hollywood and briefly ruled as the studios' favorite token-

Asian. She was gorgeous and had no business being on a city bus with a herd of migrant workers and a bum like Rex. She knew it, showed it in her blatant disregard for the needs of the elderly or pregnant.

The bus crawled through Koreatown traffic. When it stopped at Western, three young men got on. They were dressed roughly the same—gaudy tennis shoes, black and yellow, with the laces removed and the tongues pushed forward, as though their feet were talking to you as they walked. Expensive winter jackets with the Pitts-burgh Steelers logo on the back helped cover their midsections, left exposed by sagging Levis. They were wanna-be "gangstas," rich kids intent on embarrassing their parents by landing in jail for something a real Blood or Crip would never be dumb enough to try in public. As soon as they saw the Korean woman, they were on a mis-sion. They gathered around her, hanging on to the bar overhead.

One of the thuglets rubbed a tiny tuft of hair on his chin he no doubt thought was a beard. His head bobbed, like he was on a used car lot and had found exactly what he was looking for. "Damn baby," he said, "for an Asian bitch, you got some fine-ass titties." His friends jumped up and down and gave each other the latest version of "high-five."

One of them said, "But Asian bitches ain't got no booties. What about you, boo? You got something worth a train?" He tried to push the woman sideways. She slapped his hand.

"Bus driver," she said. Her English was beyond broken

and her lack of volume betrayed her lack of confidence.

The driver glanced in his giant rearview mirror. He was an older Latino with wrinkles carved so deep into his face he looked like he might slump over and die. "Leave the lady alone." His voice carried the conviction of a slug.

The Korean woman beat on the aluminum divider between her and the driver. "Bus driver!"

"You can move to the back," he said.

Encouraged, for reasons that wouldn't make sense just about anywhere else in the world, the trio of Romeos closed in on her. The two on the outside rested their palms on the windows, arching over her. The urban pillow talk continued, one thuglet after the next revealing his tender feelings for her:

"I'd hit that shit all night."

"*Yeah, boy*!"

"Goddamn, them titties look like planets!"

"*Yeah, yeah*!"

"Damn, she got herself a booty, too!"

"*Hell yeah*!"

"You can put a drink and ashtray on that shit, know what I'm saying?"

"*Aw, yeah*!"

And so on.

Rex sighed. The other passengers stared down or out the closest window. They had the same expression he saw when folks passed him on the street while he was asking for change, the expression of zombies, oblivious to anything other than what they might eat for dinner while they watched *Dancing with the Stars* or some other million-dollar piece of crap on television. He didn't care about the woman so much. He wanted the money in her purse and if somebody didn't pry the posers off of her, she might exit the bus in a place without any alleys he could drag her into. There was a desolate, residential stretch of Wilshire between Rossmore and La Brea. Impossible to rob someone there. For whatever reason, people who lived in houses were more observant. Rex waited for someone, the bus driver, the half-dozen Mexican guys who worked for a living and could easily have taken on the teenagers, anybody, to step forward and tell the kids to knock it off. He rolled his eyes. *But I'm the bad guy...*

When he was nineteen, he was the starting halfback at Texas Christian. His first two games he rushed for a total of five-hundred and twelve yards and seven touchdowns. Early in the third contest, after a week of signing copies of *Sports Illustrated* with his picture on the cover, he broke his leg handing the ball off on an end-around. A linebacker didn't notice the receiver was carrying the football and folded Rex in two. He remembered seeing a fragment of his tibia poking through his skin and then waking up in the hospital feeling as though someone had sawed on his knee and left the wound open. When the doctors confirmed he would never play ball again, the university withdrew his scholarship. He took to drinking Johnnie Walker while he worked his way through technical school. In those days, it was the best way to kill the lingering pain in his leg and his imagination, which refused to abandon the fantasy that someday he would get a second chance at a career in the NFL. By the time he received his certificate in computer programming, the habit of being drunk ensured he would never hold a job for more than a week.

And now he was here. LA. Homeless.

The Korean woman had had enough. She swung her purse and screeched "*Sheba-nom! Sheba-nom!*" until the teenagers took a step backwards. She shoved through them the way Rex once plowed through defensive lines. She pushed passengers standing in the aisle out of her way in search of another seat. As she passed them, she tried to force eye contact. None obliged. *Los Angeles, home of the toughest cowards on the planet.* The woman approached him. Her nostrils flared. She settled on a bench opposite the rear door.

"Yo, bitch," one of the young men said, "didn't nobody say you could move." He nodded to his buddies and they marched to the middle of the bus.

Balanced on the inside corner of the woman's left eye, a tear wobbled, threatened to reveal how insulted she was. She drew in her lips, took a deep breath, and pulled up her nose. The combination allowed her to rub her eyes. When her hands returned to her purse, her makeup had smeared downward. She no longer looked like the privileged wife of a Korean banker. A few alterations to her schoolgirl skirt and she could have passed for a Goth.

"You know you want what we got." The thuglet unzipped his pants. He showed her exactly what he was talking about.

"*Nam chang*!" she screamed.

The bus driver spoke up. "Do I need to call the police?" This seemed to satisfy the other passengers. They shifted their glances from the floor to the closest window or the opposite, depending on where their eyes had previously been locked. The gentlemen engaging the woman in what was inching closer and closer to a gang rape ignored the warning. The bus driver produced a cell phone, showed it to the thuglets. "You think I'm joking?"

"Shut the fuck up," said one of them.

Rex just wanted to drink himself into the blackness. He just wanted to forget, for another twenty-four hours, what a vicious joke his life was. The door to his con-science, however, creaked on its hinges.

The young men cornered the woman in her seat once again and took turns putting their hands on her. As one grabbed her breasts, another squeezed her ass. They paused to give each other "play," and continued molest-ing her. As for the woman, she must have lost all desire to look tough. Tears somersaulted down her cheeks. She choked on sobs rising from her throat in rhythmic heaves.

Rex clamped his teeth together. *Dammit.* As far as he was concerned, any woman dressed the way the Korean woman was dressed should arm herself for *precisely* this kind of attack. What really bothered him, though, was the apathy of everyone else on the bus.

One of the thuglets put his hand up the woman's skirt and attempted to yank her panties off.

Rex stood. "What the *hell* is the matter with you people?"

The passengers bowed their heads. They refused to respond in any other way. The thuglets made no such show.

"You talking to us?"

"Actually," Rex said, "I was addressing everyone but you."

The bus driver bounced his eyes into the rearview mirror. "Sit down, mister. I'll call the police at the next stop."

"Yo, man," said one of the thuglets, "why don't you mind your own damn business?"

"I am." Rex stepped away from his seat. He clenched his fists and approached the young men.

The teenagers eased off from the woman, ready to fight.

The bus stopped and the back door hissed. The Korean woman kicked her boots into the legs of the young man directly in front of her. She swung her purse at him. When he ducked, she charged forward, stumbled out and onto the street, and ran as fast as her high heels would allow. Rex glared at the young men and said, "You little jerk-offs just cost me my dinner."

The thuglets found their collective spine and descended on him. He felt six bony fists pummel him until the warmth of his own blood coated his face and he blacked out.

Two EMTs hoisted Rex onto a stretcher. The remaining passengers, the ones who had no choice but to stay on the bus, stared at him. Their frowns didn't claw him any different than the majority of the sour faces he witnessed every day on the streets. No matter what he did, he was an inconvenience to the clones who resented him because he didn't have bills to pay, mortgages to settle, children to tend, pots of stew to serve by seven or suffer the wrath of an unreasonable spouse.

As the paramedics carried him down the steps of the rear door, the gurney tilted and he slid off. He hit his head on the curb and nearly blacked out a second time. The men dressed in blue, medical jumpsuits laughed.

They took their time putting him back on the stretcher and extending the wheels. As they rolled him to an ambulance, he noticed the bus had stopped next to a liquor store. Giant words, painted in red on the side of the building, "Beer! Spirits!" floated by, like an advertisement suspended from heaven. Then he felt the reconstructed landscape of his face, round welts, some open, stinging to the touch. *I must look like a map of Mars.* It would be at least five days before he would be able to collect money without scaring off normal folks. His stomach turned and he wondered if he could even make it that long without a drink.

"American Chivalry" first appeared in *Grift.*

DUMB SHIT

Donny was the one what noticed the Mexican first. He said, "Smitty, you see him?" I followed the aim of his finger out the windshield.

A runt, if you asked me. Maybe five-two. White T-shirt and jeans, just like all them illegals wore. Sort of rubbed it in how they was doing the jobs we used to do.

"Yeah, I see him."

The Mexican was walking down Thompson Boulevard, an off-shoot of Raymond Avenue. Majority of the streetlamps was busted. There was some railroad tracks what weren't hardly used no more. Tall, dead grass here and there. Mostly patches of dirt. Looming over it all was factories what closed when we was still in high school. Places our dads worked at. If it weren't for the Mexican's bright shirt, Donny might of never spotted him.

"You think he's one of the beaners from the site?"

"The hell would I know?"

"Shit, brother, you were there."

He was talking about that morning, about our gig at a cookie-cutter development in Greenwood. A five-minute neighborhood with manicured lawns covering up what

37

used to be farms. We was supposed to get twenty-eight an hour for fixing roofs onto the houses. That was a wage set during them days we still had unions. Jimbo Pincer, the contractor, told us the Mexicans was willing to work for ten dollars an hour.

Donny threatened to grab his hunting knife what his Pa give him just before he went to Pendleton for man-slaughter. Said he'd slice Jimbo's throat open, bleed him all over the fresh blacktop.

"You threatening me?" Jimbo said.

"What do you think?" Donny said.

I had to struggle to get him back to his Ford. It was one thing to lose another job to the Mexicans. Sure as shit didn't need to go to the pokey on the count of a no-good contractor.

Soon as we was on the road, he called me a pussy for keeping him from killing Jimbo. Having known Donny my whole life, I couldn't think of him as anything but a friend. Times like that, however, I got to wondering why I put up with his dumb shit. I shrugged it off. Same as I done since we was kids. Plus, he was bigger and weren't past kicking my ass to make a point. My mind was fixed on deeper issues anyway. Tricia, my old lady, was going to have to sell her pussy to make our bills. Again. Weren't no choice. What I said to Donny was:

"Don't you think *they* want us to stomp that fucker into dust? So *they* can put us in the gas chamber?"

Donny was obsessed with Ruby Ridge and Waco and considered the Unabomber his hero. Read all manner of conspiracy books. Felt the government had been took over by something unseen and Satanic. Straight out of a horror movie. *Invasion of the Body Snatchers*, the good one with Donald Sutherland, or maybe that Roddy Piper masterpiece, *They Live*. Didn't take long for him to grab the conspiracy ball and roll with it—"Hell yeah," he said. "What do you think they refurbished the train depot in Beech Grove for? They're building concentration camps for working class Christians."

It didn't make no kind of difference that Donny hadn't been to church since he was five or six years old. Set him to weaving tapestries of Uncle Sam's connivance with Big Business and Socialists and Wicca and Area 51 and all hell else and you could guarantee he'd forget whatever happened five minutes previous.

He turned on to Thompson and crept behind the Mexican. "Baseball bats are still in the bed," he said.

I had forgot about them.

After leaving the job site that morning, we did what we always did when a contractor hired Mexicans without telling us—we went to the Body Shop to watch the daughters of girls we grew up with shake their titties for rent. We was sitting at Pervert's Row, stuffing money down the panties of a gal named Theresa. Her mom and Tricia was good friends. Donny was on his fifth bottle of Bud and probably pulled some crystal up his snout one of the ten times he went to the pisser. Point being, he was twisted and decided he was going to join Theresa on the stage and dry hump her. Didn't take Bonks, the bouncer, more than ten seconds to bull across the room and tear him off her. Bonks was built like a VW bug set on its rear end. One of the only sons of bitches what could tell Donny or me what to do and get away with it.

"You boys going to settle or hit the damn road," he said. He directed that to me as well, which weren't too cool considering I weren't the one engaged in dumb shit. I let it drift, though, mostly because Bonks was my brother-in-law.

Donny, who had known Bonks since high school, said he would get his hunting knife and slash his throat open and bleed him right there on the stage. That got the both of us thrown out. "We're going to my place," he said. "Going to get my son's baseball bats, come back here and cripple that goddamn mutant."

I did my best to talk him out of it on the way to Fountain Square. He pulled into his gravel driveway. Called me a pussy and told me to shut the fuck up. As he went inside to get the bats, I noticed he hadn't cut his lawn in a while. When he returned, he stomped across the high grass with two aluminum sluggers and tossed them onto the bed of the truck.

As he drove us to Madison Avenue, toward the Body Shop once more, I finally convinced him to let it go. "Why don't we check up on Tammy and Heather over at the Silk 'N' Lace?" I said. Now, the Silk was one of the most disgusting strip joints in the city. Grass was so high it had sort of taken over the parking lot. Inside, it weren't unusual to see rats hopping across the floor, picking at peanut droppings. The dancers was either junkies or preggers. For a dollar, you could get them to squeeze titty milk on you. Donny loved that sort of shit. He agreed to head there and mellow. We tossed what cash we had at middle-aged women what never figured out a different way to make their bills until the sun set. Until we was drunk enough to face our wives and explain why they was going to have to pull twice their weight. Again.

That's when Donny saw the Mexican.

I searched for an excuse to get him and his Ford back on Raymond, back in the direction of Fountain Square. "You want to be pissed at somebody," I said, "get pissed at Jimbo Pincer. He's the son of a bitch what hired us and then brought scabs in to cut our wages."

The truck came to a stop. Donny said, "You sound like one of them fruity kids from IUPUI that's always trying to rationalize amnesty for these goddamn invaders." He switched on the dome light and squinted at me. "You haven't been cloned or something, have you?"

The kind of shit he often came up with went a long way toward explaining why every movie or television show I ever seen depicted poor folk like us as the dumbest fuckers in the universe. All I could say was, "*Man...*"

"Let's go," he said. He jumped out his side, walked around the back and grabbed the baseball bats. When he got to my door, he ripped it open and pulled me by my arm from the truck onto the street. He shoved one of the bats at me. "Take it, brother."

By then, the Mexican noticed us. Stood still. Hands in his pockets.

"Donny, you don't know who he is," I said. "Could be legal, could be a family man what got nothing to do with them Mexicans at the site today."

He started in the Mexican's direction.

The Mexican didn't move. Maybe he was afraid. Maybe the complete opposite.

Donny saw I was loitering on the street. He waved me over, said, "Let's go, pussy."

What I wanted to do was run in the other direction. That would have branded me for the rest of my days. Would have forced me to move somewhere else. So I chased after him, mostly to talk him out of whatever dumb shit he had in mind. When I got a good look at the Mexican, I said, "This ain't one of them scabs."

"That doesn't matter. Not now, brother."

I said the only thing I figured might turn his intentions—"You want to go to Pendleton, like your dad? Over someone you don't even know?"

The Mexican said: "What you want?" He spit on the sidewalk in front of him, like a border he dared us to cross.

Donny slammed his baseball bat into the Mexican's knee. The Mexican collapsed. He screamed and shouted, "*Pendejo!*" Donny hit him in the same spot and we heard a *pop*. This made the Mexican grab his leg and squirm. The purple reflection of the nearest street lamp weaved down his face in tears.

When Donny drew back to hit him again, I grabbed his hand. "Ain't that enough?"

I let go and he hoisted the bat over his head, aiming

for me.

"Come on, Donny."

The Mexican stopped making noise.

Between clenched teeth, Donny said, "The fuck you say my name for?" He tapped the baseball bat in my hand. "Take a swing."

I shook my head.

He grinned and nodded.

I shook my head again.

"You're taking swipes at this piece of shit or I'm leaving two corpses for the rats."

"I ain't going to jail. Not over a Mexican."

He smiled. "Nobody gives a damn about a goddamn illegal."

When I didn't move, Donny smashed his baseball bat into my side. "Swing, you goddamn pussy!"

I blasted the Mexican in his chest, over and over. If my conscience crept up, trying to sneak a word in, I lied and said it was Jimbo Pincer I was beating into hamburger meat.

Donny joined me, bashing the Mexican all over. Every hit made a different noise. I thought of that old cereal commercial, *Snap Crackle Pop!* We turned the Mexican into a twitching bundle of bloodied clothes. Eventually, he stopped moving. I figured we killed him. When I said so, Donny said he didn't care.

We kick-rolled the body into the tall grass and dumped the bats near it.

* * *

Got a call from Donny the next morning. Cops had already been to his place. Found two blood-stained DeMarini bats with his son's initials etched into the bottom of the handles. The Mexican weren't dead, he said. In a coma. Wouldn't never walk again. He chuckled about that, claimed it served the Mexican right for taking our jobs.

"Here's what I told them," he said. Then he explained the story he'd come up with. How the Mexican had attacked us. "They tried to get me to turn on you, brother. Promised they'd keep me out of the pokey if I testified it was all your idea." He assured me he did no such thing. Stuck to his self-defense story until the cops gave up and left.

He insisted I do the same.

Tricia shouted my name from the living room. I heard the knock on the door while I was still on the phone, heard the door open, heard the official voices of at least two detectives. "Don't you worry about a thing," I said to Donny.

As I made my way down the hallway, the spiffy cops came into view. Standing next to them was my wife, still in the pink sweat pants and WWF T-shirt she wore to bed. Dirty blonde hair shooting every which way. Had that look on her face like she was fixed on telling me what my next move was. I felt a relief I ain't ever felt before.

"Dumb Shit" first appeared in *Indiana Crime 2012*.

SPARE CHANGE

She pulled it out of her purse. Slowly, cautiously, always looking around, making sure I was the only one who could see it. She said it was a .32. I believed her. Just as quickly as she showed it to me, she shoved it back in between a plastic bundle of tissues and what appeared to be a thin red wallet.

"*That's* why I'm drinking like this, mister." She chased her words with a shot of whiskey. Her fifth, by my count.

"You aiming that at anyone in particular?" I said.

She twisted her face.

"Boyfriend?"

"Husband."

"Lied to you?"

"That one's on the list." She smacked the bar, gestured for the man pouring drinks to fill her glass again.

"Ain't you had enough, little lady?" The bartender must not have been aware of the gun in her purse.

"Just do your job," she said.

He shrugged and dropped another shot in front of her.

"What'd your old man do?" I said.

She gave me a long look. Up and down. She shrugged. She'd already showed me the gun. I guess she supposed she might as well hook a story on it. "He wanted five kids," she said. "I've given him three. You have any idea what it takes to raise one?"

I nodded. I had a son and daughter and ran out on their mother when the bills got to be too much. These days I sent her a little money here and there, but to a lazy thief like me, putting bread on my own table was a task and a half. It's not that I wanted to hurt my old lady. I had no choice. "Children can drain you," I said.

She must not have liked my siding with her. "That's putting it mildly, mister," she said. "I went from being the most desirable woman in the world to one of those worn out mamas dragging critters through the mall in search of diapers and socks and lunch boxes and crayons." She stopped. Long enough to have another shot.

"Sometimes men don't notice the sacrifices women make." Probably should have kept my mouth shut.

The woman laughed. "If they were giving out prizes for understatements, mister, you would have it." She raised her empty glass for a silent toast.

The bartender set the bottle in front of her and walked away.

I said, "I've never won a damn thing in my life."

"What do you do for a living?" she asked.

I could tell she just wanted to sidetrack my interest in the .32. Since she had been so honest with me, I returned the favor. "I'm a professional thief. Gas stations and liquor stores. Nothing too glamorous."

She nodded. "Maybe we got something in common after all."

I didn't want that. "Ever been to prison?"

"Of course not."

"If you think life is rough now, just wait till they throw you over the wall."

Scooting her chair closer, she put her lips to my ear and spoke in a curt, seething voice. "Try juggling three jobs, three children, and a man that sleeps with anything that'll give him the time of day. Comes home to me, passes on two, not one, *two* diseases you can only get from loving, the kind that don't kill you, just linger there, waiting for the moment you meet someone you might like, and then, pop!, sores all over your mouth. *Marked.* And I didn't do nothing wrong. I didn't do a thing to deserve that kind of punishment."

"Ever heard of divorce? Makes these situations a lot easier to deal with."

"That sonofabitch'd never go for it. Says I belong to him. We passed on our blood together and he'll be goddamned to let me be. I tell him he can keep the damn kids if that's his issue. No, he says, he loves me too much. What about them other bitches? I ask. I don't love them, he says."

She took another shot.

"I wish you'd think about this," I said. "You're still just as pretty as can be, even if you don't feel it or recognize it, on account of how tough your life has been. All you need is a lawyer, get this situation into the legal system, the right way, that is."

She said, "I appreciate your trying to help, mister, but I can't get away from him. I've tried. He hunts me down, smacks me just hard enough to make an impression folks can't see on the outside."

I sighed. In my own way, I had been terrible to the woman who had done right by me. I sure as hell was in no position to judge anyone.

"Well," she stumbled off her bar stool, "time to set things proper." She leaned in close once more. "Promise me you won't tell nobody."

I grabbed her arm and pulled her in tighter. "I won't, angel, I just want you to do me a favor. Think real hard about what you're fixed on doing. Think about it as you leave here. If you decide on a more, shall we say, legitimate road toward ridding yourself of the bum, leave the gun in the trash can outside, the green one under the Budweiser sign in the window. I'll take care of it, drop it somewhere they'll never trace back to you."

Maybe she wasn't interested in being saved, maybe I reminded her of her father, or worse, her husband. She yanked herself away and rushed out the door.

I didn't watch her go. I ordered a drink. Then another. Then I settled up, put on my coat and headed for the door.

Outside the bar, the lid on the green trash can had been moved. My heart beat a little faster. I opened it and looked inside.

The gun wasn't there.

Pulling my coat in tighter, I walked into the night

looking for a liquor store to knock over. I got the register at the Bottle Stop, on Forty-ninth Street. The idiot clerk honestly didn't know how to open the safe. I let it ride.

I counted the money as I entered a Western Union a few blocks to the north. Just under three bills. I gave the clerk on duty my wife's address and shoved all the dough across the counter. I used some spare change in my pocket to pay the delivery fee.

"Spare Change," originally titled "Diseases from Loving," first appeared in *Beat to a Pulp*.

STATE ROAD 53

One

"Bud?"

"Yeah?"

"Tell Lynn I want to see her."

Bud sighed.

Ron felt bad for him. The entire town knew what was happening while Bud worked the night shift at Liberty Steel. He sounded glummer than usual. Ron figured it was on account of the strike. Bud Gorski couldn't satisfy his wife and now his bosses refused to pay him what he was worth. Ron thought he was a good guy. He made it possible for Lynn to raise their boys without her having to get a job. Most important, he understood he just didn't have the gump to give her what she needed in bed.

Ron didn't consider himself an especially skilled lover. He figured the demon energy he brought back from three tours in the jungle provided animal attributes Lynn mistook for prowess. Whatever the reasons, he tried to keep things cordial with Bud. He didn't want to see the twins grow up without their father. Nothing had ever been officially spoken. Bud worked the graveyard shift in the mill Monday through Friday. Two or three nights during the week, Deputy Sheriff Ronald Quinn went to work on Bud's wife.

Bud said he'd pass the message. "You going to wait until I'm gone?"

"Sure thing." Ron hung up. He went back to his cruiser and started for the north side of town. He radioed the station. Nobody answered. He figured Beth, the night dispatch, had fallen asleep. No big deal. Haggard hadn't seen any serious crime since the 1930s, before Ron had been born. Occasionally, a carload of teenagers from Gary drifted too far south on State Road 53 and him or Sherriff Dudek would pull them over and remind them, in a manner most friendly, that they couldn't possibly have any business in a nice town like Haggard.

He parked across the street from Bud Gorski's one-story house on Old Ridge Road. It was protected by a thin sheet of painted aluminum and had a small, covered stoop with three steps leading to the front door. Just like every other house on the block. Ron smoked an unfiltered Pall Mall while he waited.

Bud stepped out and crossed his snow-covered lawn with a picket sign and lunch pail under his arm. He unlocked the back door to his Chevelle and tossed them in. Then he opened the front and glanced over. From across the street, Ron could see any remaining enthusiasm Bud had for life drop right out of his eyes.

* * *

Lynn Gorski answered the door in a pink nightie. She had her dusty-blonde hair up in a beehive. Ron thought of the covers of fashion magazines he had seen at Union Station in Chicago. Women in big cities had already abandoned that style. Didn't matter. He'd have her hair down and wrapped around his fist soon enough. "Twins asleep?"

"Of course." Her voice quaked. "I'm glad you called." She grabbed his ear with her teeth and slid her tongue around the rim. "Don't ever make me wait a whole week again." Her fingers marched down his chest and unfastened his gun belt. She almost let it drop. He caught it and pushed her away.

"Take it easy, baby," he said. His gun clanked on the round table in the kitchen as he set the belt on it. Crusted spaghetti sauce stained three of four flower-patterned placemats laid out.

Lynn stood back. She brushed her hand along her forehead. "I'm cool."

"The hell you are," he said. "Can I get a beer?"

She nodded at the fridge.

Ron found a can of Schlitz. He peeled the lid off and tossed the tab into a rubber trash can by the sink.

Lynn walked toward the bedroom. "I changed the sheets before Bud left."

"Probably should of waited." He took a noisy swig.

"Nothing we can do about it now." Lynn stood in the doorway, resting against the frame. Her fingers marched up her thigh, pushing her gown higher and higher.

Ron finished his beer and approached her, unbuttoning his shirt along the way.

"How was work?" she asked.

"Boring."

"Same old same old?"

Ron and Lynn lay in bed. They shared a cigarette. She said something about going to Chicago together. He sighed. "You know that ain't going to happen."

She wrapped her legs around him. Running her fingers in the cross-pattern on his chest, then down to the left, where a small chunk had been taken from him when a VC shot him in the side, she said, "You won't let nobody in."

"Lost enough people to know better." He dragged on the cigarette and passed it. "Besides, you don't ever tire of telling me how much you love Bud."

"I do love Bud. I also love you."

"That ain't even possible."

Gunshots exploded down the street. Ron grabbed Lynn and rolled her off the side of the bed. He crawled out to the hallway and into the twins' room. He woke Sam and Andrew Gorski long enough to help them from their bunk beds to the floor. "Stay low," he told them.

When he returned to the master bedroom, he stopped. Lynn stood by the window, holding a Marlin across her naked body. "It's just the intimidators," she said. "From Liberty."

Ron pointed at the gun. "That a recent addition to the family?"

She smiled. "Bud bought it after that preacher was shot in Memphis. While you were gone, you know." She looked away from him. "He was worried the riots might spill over."

Ron took the gun from her. It was loaded. "Careful, baby."

She rolled her eyes. "I grew up in Kentucky, Ronald."

He realized he missed what she said when he first returned and saw her holding the gun. "Liberty Steel?"

"They send a truck full of goons every night. Since the union ok'd the strike."

"Why ain't I heard of this?"

Lynn shrugged. "Not really police business." She got back on the bed. She lay on her side, tracing the curve of her hips with her fingertips. "Why don't you put that away?" She nodded to the shotgun.

Ron asked her where she kept it. She told him Bud's closet, on the top shelf. "Next to the box of shells."

Lynn smacked the switch on her alarm clock at seven-ten. Ron got dressed while she stayed in bed, smoking. He noticed two holes in the wall, just to the right of the window. Leaning in to get a better look, he stuck his pinky in one of them.

Lynn rested on her elbows. "They blasted this side of the street three nights ago."

"Why ain't you talking to me?"

"It's Liberty Steel, honey. They built every town in Lake County."

55

"You could get hurt."

"Bud says this'll pass when the union gets its way."

"I don't like it." Ron stuffed his shirt into his pants.

Lynn stretched her leg out and caressed him with her toes. "I appreciate your worries. Bud's got it all took care of."

Ron kissed her goodbye. He grabbed his gun belt on the way to the front door. He stepped outside just as Bud's burgundy, rusted Chevy pulled into the driveway. The two men exchanged curt nods. Ron laid tracks in fresh snow, clear across the lawn and street to his cruiser. He got in and started the engine.

Bud moped along, arched over, like a hunchback, staring at his feet. He seemed more miserable and pathetic than ever. Ron felt like saying something. He couldn't think of anything that would help.

Two

Ron parked his cruiser behind a ground-level billboard with a strawberry lollipop on it advertising Haddaker's Drug Store. Toward the front of his mind was the notion that he was looking out for the people of Haggard. On the other side was a suspicion that he was just bored. He had been in a stupor since coming home. The only physical excitement he got was from Lynn Gorski. Now he had something resembling a *mission*. What was damn clear was that nobody else in town cared about the Liberty Steel gun thugs. It didn't make sense to him. He hadn't slept since leaving the Gorski house that morning.

He caught the sheriff just before lunch, asked him if he was aware of the truck full of guns spitting bullets on Old Ridge. "Nope," said Sheriff Dudek. The old man twisted the toothpick in his mouth round and round and lowered his eyes.

Ron had done enough interrogation work in the war to know when a human being was lying to him. "Gorski house's got holes in it."

Sheriff Dudek laughed. "I thought you was plugging them holes!" He looked back at Gretchen, the daytime dispatch. She obliged with a giggle.

Ron said, "I don't think this is something we can shrug."

The sheriff stepped closer. He inflated his chest and nodded up to face the young deputy. "Things happen, as you're well aware, that the law don't have any say regarding." He turned to walk away. "Get on them roads. Write some tickets and make us some money so we can have us a nice Christmas party."

The sheriff stepped into his office and slammed the door. As Ron made his way out of the station, Gretchen stopped him. "You're fortunate to come back in one piece, Ronald," she said. "Don't be stupid. Not now."

He thanked her and left. While he ate a hot dog and soft-serve cone for lunch, watching icicles melt off the gutters of the Dairy Queen in downtown Haggard, he decided he would chase the truck by himself and arrest the whole lot. "I like to see them suits cross 53 explain themselves." He thought of *Rio Bravo*, his favorite movie when he was a kid. He thought about how John

Wayne might have handled the situation.

He almost fell asleep, waiting there in the dark for the truck. The sound of a larger vehicle, struggling in the cold, cut through the country silence. He sat up to crank the ignition on his Ford. A blood-colored Dodge Power Wagon rumbled past him. He turned the key but the engine wouldn't fire.

"Dammit!"

Guns went off down the road. Glass broke, women screamed, and doors opened and slammed. Ron got the cruiser started and tore out from behind the billboard. His wheels spun on packed snow. He straightened the car and flipped his sirens on.

The Ford roared up behind the truck. There were four men in the back wearing potato sacks over their heads with half-dollar-sized holes cut for their eyes. Two of them aimed their shotguns at Ron. The thug closest to the cab beat on the rear window and motioned for the driver to step on it. The muffler coughed black smoke as the Dodge mustered speed. It continued on Old Ridge and nearly tipped as it veered right, onto State Road 53.

Ron put his foot on the gas and the Ford threatened to fly past the truck when he whipped the steering-wheel. The pick-up fish-tailed its way over the ice-coated bridge connecting Haggard and Gary. There were no rails and the men in the back braced themselves for the possibility of going over the side and plunging into Lake Arthur. Ron slowed down. The truck gained a mile on him by the time he was across.

He chased them up 53, passing white fields outside of

Industry Row, where nine companies employed most of the labor in Lake County. Smokestacks curled smog into the sky twenty-four hours a day. The entire town smelled like rotten eggs.

A Gary Municipal flashed its sirens and zoomed in front of Ron. The driver tapped the brakes, forcing him to pull over. The officers stepped out of the cruiser and approached him as though he were possibly on the wrong side of the law, dancing their flashlights across his windshield. He opened his door and nudged his way out with his hands raised.

He recognized the officer who had been driving. They did basic together at Fort Harrison, down in Indianapolis, in '67. They spent the Summer of Love crawling through mud while their drill sergeant called them maggots. "What's going on, Calvin?"

"At ease, soldier. We ain't going to do you like you do our folks any time they wander into Haggard."

Ron lowered his hands. "Just don't do me like you did that Italian girl at the funhouse in Kokomo."

Calvin laughed. "I'm unaware of any such activity, nor would I say shit about it if I was." He kept his flashlight aimed at Ron. "What you doing this far north?"

"I was hoping to apprehend the men in that pick-up that passed here a few minutes ago."

The Gary officers looked at each other. They offered their best impressions of confusion and ignorance.

"We didn't see any pick-up."

Ron sighed. He was sick of people thinking he was too stupid to figure out when they were lying to him.

"You didn't see that red Dodge? There was four men in the back with shotguns, wearing masks. They looked like ghosts."

Calvin shrugged. "No idea."

Ron stepped backwards, toward his cruiser. "Mind if I drive into town and have a look?"

Calvin shook his head. "Best thing for you is to head back to Haggard."

Ron stopped.

Calvin's partner rested his free hand on his pistol.

Calvin said, "No need to go begging the Man to dig us early graves. Not after the shit we've been through."

"Lake County Sheriff's Department's got jurisdiction."

"That so?" Calvin reached down and unfastened the button keeping his gun in his holster.

Ron considered his odds. "All right," he said.

Calvin smiled. "Good seeing you, soldier."

Ron got in his car, turned around and drove slowly toward Lake Arthur. He kept an eye on the rearview, hoping Calvin and his partner would move on. They didn't.

As he approached Old Ridge Road, he saw an ambulance from St. Mary's near the Gorski house. Sheriff Dudek's car was parked across the street. Families gathered on the lawn.

He pulled up behind Sheriff Dudek's cruiser. Bud Gorski's neighbors let him know what happened. He got to the mailbox posted at the end of the driveway and stopped. The front door opened and two paramedics carried a body, covered with a white sheet, to the ambulance. The sheriff followed behind the medics. When he saw Ron, he pushed past a crowd of huddled wives.

"Where you been, Deputy?"

Ron told him.

The sheriff studied him the way his father did when he was younger, just before he got drafted and all he ever did was drink and fight and get thrown into the drunk tank. "I wonder if you had done like you was told and kept to Haggard, if Bud Gorski might be alive right now."

Ron wanted to get inside, to talk to Lynn. He tried moving around the sheriff.

"Where you headed?"

He nodded toward the house.

"Whatever for?"

Ron looked at him.

"If you was so concerned about happenings in Haggard, you sure as hell wouldn't have taken a joy ride up to Gary."

"I told you..."

The sheriff got close enough for Ron to smell Wild Turkey on his breath. "Not a thing in there needing your attention." He waited for him to stand down. Then he strolled over to his cruiser, telling regular folks there was "nothing more to gawk at."

A third paramedic helped Lynn outside. Ron strained to make eye contact with her. There were too many people between them. She seemed dazed, stumbling and twisting her head side to side, as though she was expecting another attack. She reminded him of older women in Vietnam. The ones who helped stack or bury their dead.

"Who's watching the boys?" he said.

Sheila Hyatt, who lived two doors from the Gorski's, said, "Beth's got them over at her place. Scooped them up before anybody goofed and let them know what happened."

The paramedics closed the doors on the ambulance. Lynn and her husband were taken to St. Mary's where a doctor could file the necessary papers, making Bud's death official.

Three

The morning after Bud Gorski was murdered, a knock fell on Ron's door while he was eating a bowl of Quaker Oates. He lived in a one-bedroom apartment on the second floor of the old red-bricked building Haddager's was located in. There wasn't much furniture. Just a table and a single chair to go with it and a cot he picked up from a surplus store in Chicago. He was still in his boxers. He scratched his front and back on his way to the door. As he opened it, he got the idea it was Lynn, that she had come to tell him she wanted to get married. He decided he would say yes. He wouldn't even make her sweat it.

Three men in jeans, flannel shirts, and potato sacks over their heads shoved him into his room. One of them said, "Mind yourself. He's a vet." They kicked him and punched him until he collapsed. Two of the thugs stepped on his right arm, one at the wrist, the other at his shoulder. The third man produced a tire iron.

"This here's a suggestion." He knelt down and bashed Ron's arm. When he stopped, he wiped blood off of the iron and said, "Poke your snout in the wrong place one more time. I dare you."

The men left the apartment without closing the door.

Ron caught his breath and rolled onto his left arm. He pushed himself off the ground. He would have to go down to the drug store to use their phone. Most likely, he hoped, someone would catch sight of the bone poking through his skin and call an ambulance for him.

Ron Quinn's parents split before he ever got to know his mom. While he was fighting the war, his dad got lung cancer, probably from working in the cement factory on the east side of Haggard. Most of the folks who earned a living there ended their days in hospital beds with tubes in their throats.

When he returned from the jungle, the women his age were already married. The men who had stayed behind, who had weaseled out with money or left the country, looked at him funny. They probably felt guilty. He dated Lynn in high school and when he ran into her a few days after coming home, he realized he had what she needed. He believed she could do the same for him. But her kids would never be his kids. She was hooked on something Bud provided. Maybe Bud was smarter than him. Maybe Lynn was smarter, too. Ron tossed and turned while he slept because he knew he was, and always would be, alone.

He woke up at St. Mary's. A nurse was changing bags of fluids pouring into an I.V. plugged into the back of his left hand. They must have been giving him morphine. He couldn't feel a thing. Lynn stood by the only window. He thought of the last night they had made love.

"Hey baby," he said. His throat felt like it was filled with rocks.

She drifted over and ran her fingers along his right arm, which was covered in a cast. "We're putting Bud in the ground tomorrow," she said. "Catholic funeral."

Ron said, "I'll be there."

"Doubt they'll let you loose from here that soon."

He asked her what had happened. She explained that they were asleep when the shooting started. She said Bud's blood sprayed her face and the bullet angled off into their headboard. Then she asked, "Who did this to you?"

"Pretty sure it was the same people."

"Figured so."

He told her how he chased the gun thugs to Gary.

"State Road 53?"

"What you thinking about, Lynn?"

"Nothing." She turned away from him.

Another goddamn liar.

Lynn stayed with him until the nurses kicked her out. They sneered when they spoke to her. Ron told them to back off. When she was gone, the head nurse whispered, "You two are going *straight* to hell."

* * *

Ron was released from the hospital two days later. He missed Bud Gorski's funeral. Sheriff Dudek told him to take it easy. The last thing Ronald Quinn wanted, though, was more time to himself. He went back to work the next day with a bottle of Darvocet hidden in his glove box. The sheriff called him to his office.

"You clear, now?" He nodded toward a wooden chair on the other side of his desk.

Ron declined the offer to sit. "What do you mean?"

"Your job is to write tickets and chase the coloreds back up to Gary. You ain't Mickey Spillane. You ain't Sam Spade. And you sure as hell ain't no hero. Confine yourself to Haggard, or find another way to pay your bills."

Neither man spoke for a moment. Then the sheriff repeated his first question.

Ron thought he was stupid for even asking. The strike would be over, regardless of how it turned out for Liberty or the workers, long before his arm mended. He assured the sheriff he wasn't going to do anything but burn fuel, driving round and round Haggard city limits.

He parked in the lot of the Dairy Queen that night to take a nap. The air outside was freezing. He rolled the windows up and turned the heater on. The speaker on his police radio crackled and the night dispatch told him to get to the bridge on State Road 53.

He flipped his lights on and raced over ice-coated roads. He passed Old Ridge and got a feeling things were never going to be the same. When he drove up to Lake Arthur and the iron bridge, there were a dozen squad cars from three different police agencies gathered, lights turning. Police walked off the side and down a slope toward the water. His eyes followed them. There was more activity by the shore. He parked and got out. The ground was slick from a sheer layer of ice.

Sheriff Dudek stood among a group of Gary Municipal officers. Ron approached him. "What's going on?"

The sheriff directed his attention to the frozen lake, just beyond the edge of the bridge. A crane was hoisting a red pick-up truck from a crater in the ice. "Where you been tonight?"

"Minding my own."

The sheriff said he believed him.

The officers examining the truck made their way to the top of the bridge. One of them explained, "Front tires was shot out."

Sheriff Dudek took him aside. "Bud Gorski have any guns in his house?"

Ron stuttered. "Doesn't everybody?"

The sheriff raised his chin and smiled. "Go get the Gorski broad. Bring her to the station."

Ron moped back to his cruiser. He remembered Bud walking the very same way. He got in the Ford, fired it up, turned around and drove toward Old Ridge Road.

Most of the cars on the street were frosted over. The

ice on Bud's Chevelle had been cleared. Pieces of it were still breaking off and sliding down the windows. Ron parked in the driveway, to the side of Bud's car. He approached the front door with his .38 already drawn, wondering if Lynn Gorski had it in her to shoot him. He knocked and waited.

She let him in. She was wearing her coat and the twins were seated on the dull yellow couch in the living room, dressed in matching parkas. He looked at his watch. It was after midnight. "You fixing on taking the boys out for a milkshake?"

She opened her mouth to speak, but said nothing. He crossed the room and noticed she was trying to hide three suitcases standing in the narrow hallway between the bedrooms. He pretended he wasn't aware of them.

"I just wanted to see the damage from the…" He glanced back at the boys. "Well, you know what I'm getting at."

She remained still. He slid past her and into the bedroom. He knelt down and studied the hole in the wall caused by the shot that killed Bud. He stood up and approached Bud's open closet. The gun rested on the shelf where it was supposed to be. The box of shells was turned on its side. Empty.

Lynn stood in the doorway, staring at him.

He reached up and took the Marlin down. "Baby," he said. He closed his eyes. When he opened them again, she was gone.

The front door slammed shut.

Ron Quinn took a deep breath. He put his finger in

the hole in the wall across from the bed. Then he counted, "One Mississippi, two Mississippi..." At three Mississippi, he heard the engine on the Chevy rev. Ice cracked like thunder as the wheels rolled over it. He put the shotgun down and moseyed out of the house.

He got in his cruiser and casually turned the sirens on. He took his time backing up and taking off after Lynn Gorski and her sons. He kept a good distance between them so that she wouldn't panic and crash. She was smart and took Thirty-fifth Avenue to I-65. He followed her onto the highway and made sure she crossed the Illinois state line. He slowed down and watched the Chevy's tail lights thin to darkness, hoping she'd have the sense to go all the way to Canada. Then he made a U-turn and drove back to Haggard. He grimaced, like he had bit into something awful, and rehearsed the lie he would tell to guarantee he never saw Lynn Gorski again.

"State Road 53" first appeared in *Beat to a Pulp: Round Two*.

PATIENCE

I didn't normally go for blondes. I liked the dark-haired girls. Didn't matter what ethnicity. Asian, White, Latina, whatever. But this broad, she walked in, sat down right next to me. Bleach-blonde. Matched the color her eyes turned anytime they caught what little light there was in the joint. I could tell by the way she dressed she was hooking for a living. Mini-skirt, six-inch heels, a halter-top so tight I wondered how she could breathe. That didn't bother me.

"My name is Patience," she said. She shifted her legs in her sparkly little skirt. She did it slowly, giving me no choice but to watch and enjoy.

And I did.

She stuck out her hand in a half-dainty manner, like the streets hadn't stripped her of an ounce of civility. I offered a sloppy shake, glancing past her, attempting to feign disinterest. "Stan Dillon," I said.

"Stan," she said. She scooted as close to me as possible, making sure her legs brushed against mine. "What's a stud like you doing all alone on a Friday night?"

I shrugged, looked at the neon Budweiser clock hanging over the bottles behind the bar. "Nothing better to do, I guess."

"You a cop?" she said.

I nodded.

"You on duty?"

I shook my head.

"You guys make a lot of money, don't you?"

I howled. "Hey Travis," I said, "Patience here thinks I'm rolling in the green."

The bartender tossed up his phony, Ed McMahon laugh and went back to counting change in the register.

"I'll bet you make enough to satisfy me," Patience said. She ran a finger down my thigh and then stuck it in her mouth.

"Is that right?" I said.

She leaned in close, breathed fire into my ear and whispered, "How'd you like to get down with two girls tonight?"

Wouldn't have been nothing new for me. In fact, my second wife, Angela, left me precisely because I had got trapped in a sting the *LA Times* put together. A jackass investigative reporter busted in and snapped pictures of me and two Korean hookers in a massage parlor on La Brea. That was the reason the court didn't give a damn about my side of the story.

"Sure," I said.

"My friend Finesse will meet us at the Ramada on Wilshire."

* * *

We drove a long time without conversation. Through Skid Row, past Little Tokyo, across Third and into the Rampart district. Canyons of lit up buildings from downtown to Koreatown. Patience put the car radio on KJAZ and whistled to tunes she'd obviously never heard before. Finally, I said, "So when'd you get to LA?"

"What's it matter?"

A light rain made me concentrate more on the road than the conversation. I said, "I've never seen you at the 4200 before."

She stared out the window. "Finesse just told me about that joint. Said there were Johnnies there who were cool with girls like us." She pulled a makeup kit out of her fake leopard skin purse and went to work on her face. My cop instincts started making tiny noises in the back of my head. I got to thinking I'd met her before.

"Have I ever busted you?" I said.

She shook her head. "Never been in the tank," she said. "Not for this, at least."

"It's just that sometimes I arrest a girl and she tries to get revenge by setting me up. I got to be safe, you know?"

"A little paranoid?" she said.

"This is LA," I said, "land of flakes with a vendetta against the cops. You wouldn't believe how many times these corrupt media people try to make us look bad."

"Relax, honey," she said, "I just want to have some fun." She put her hand on my leg.

My cop instincts settled down. She was tiny. If she tried to pull something, I could overpower her easy enough, snuff her if I had to and dump her body somewhere in the Toy District. Nobody would notice in time. If they did ID her, nobody would care.

Whenever I got to thinking like that, I thought about how much I wanted to just kill myself. I had seen enough human garbage and enough humans being treated like garbage that I had lost faith in the idea that anything in this world was good. Sometimes I put my Glock in my mouth, closed my eyes, and imagined pulling the trigger. Maybe I was too much of an egomaniac to do it. Maybe, somewhere in my stinking head, I thought something would happen and people would change and the world would change with them. Then I usually had a drink to cover up all those ideas. Last thing LAPD needed was a cop with a soul.

I focused on Patience's legs. She couldn't have been more than twenty-seven or twenty-eight. She did a pretty good job hiding her age, but too much time in the sun gave it away. The spider webs had started to form at the far corners of her eyes. Her neck was already sagging just a bit. In two years she would be, in the eyes of shallow, materialist Los Angeles, way over the hill.

"What are you thinking about?" she asked.

I shook off all the negative crap in my head, forced myself to smile. "I'm wondering how much I'm going to enjoy tonight." As soon as I said it, I believed it.

She rested her head on my shoulder, just like she was a normal human being.

* * *

72

Patience made sure I brought my handcuffs with me up to her room. That didn't bother me one bit. As soon as she closed the door, she was all over me. Clawing at my clothes, licking my face like I was a lollipop. "Get this out of here," she said, tugging at my shirt. She nearly ripped the buttons off pulling it over my head.

"All right, all right," I said, pushing her off of me. I took my undershirt off and threw it on the bed. I tried to remove her skirt. She slapped my hands away.

"You first," she said, unbuckling my belt.

"Where's, ah, your friend?" I helped her with my pants.

"Finesse will be here when it's time," she said. "She's not into foreplay."

Had she not been running her hands in and out of my boxers, I might have asked more, *better* questions.

"Let's go!" she said. She dragged my shorts to my ankles and shoved me backwards onto the bed.

At that point I was laughing. The whole thing was absurd. This little woman, pushing around Big Bad Johnny Law. She yanked my socks off and jumped on top of me. She squeezed my waist between her thighs, surrounded me with her warmth, and snaked down and almost kissed me. I reached for her with my lips but she raised back up and, without my taking much notice, grabbed my wrists and guided them behind the steel bars at the head of the bed.

Then the cuffs, *my* cuffs, were on my hands.

"Hey, baby," I said, "I'm, you know, quite at a loss here."

She put her finger over my mouth. "Be cool."

I didn't say a thing as she used my socks to tie my legs to the posts at the foot of the bed. Then she corkscrewed like an old movie star on those high heels to the bathroom. I thought she might be throwing on something even sexier. Then I heard her talking to someone behind the door. She spoke in a soothing, tender voice, the way one might speak to an anxious child.

When she came back out, she had a jar of peanut butter and a spatula in her hands.

"*Whoa,*" I said. "I'm thinking this is gonna get pretty kinky."

"You're thinking right, mister." She sat on the bed next to me. She opened the jar and scooped out a heap of peanut butter.

"What's the plan?"

She smiled. She smeared the peanut butter all over my chest. It was sticky and warm and, to be honest, didn't turn me on all that much.

"Really, Patience," I said, "what do you got in mind here?"

Something rattled in the bathroom. "That your friend?"

"I told you," she said, "Finesse will be here when the time is right." She continued spreading peanut butter all over my body.

"I sure hope you got a clever way to remove this," I said, using my chin to point at the sea of brown gunk.

She stuck out her tongue and winked at me. "Didn't I say this would be a night you would never forget?"

When she was finally out of peanut butter, she put

the jar on the floor. Then she stood and pulled her blond hair off of her head. Underneath, wouldn't you know it, she was a brunette. My favorite.

"You remember me now?" she said.

I closed my eyes and asked a God I didn't really believe in how I could have been so stupid. "No," I said, still not looking at her. "When did I arrest you and what was it for?"

"You didn't."

I opened my eyes.

"When I was thirteen, you offered me a ride home from school. Virgil Junior High, on Vermont."

One of many sealed capsules of guilt opened in the pit of my stomach. "Jesus," I said, "that was, like, fifteen years ago."

She nodded.

"I'm sorry," I said. "I forgot all about it. Whatever it is that happened, I forgot."

"I didn't," she said. Her eyes got wider. I could almost see what she would have looked like as a child. "Hard to forget losing your virginity to a flashlight."

At first, I failed to recognize that I had started to cry. Maybe I knew things were about to get much, much worse. "Sweetheart," I said, "you can't hold me responsible for the way I acted back then."

She hissed, loud enough to shut me up. Before I could regroup and protest once more, she slid her panties down her legs from under her skirt and stuffed them into my mouth. "It's time for you to meet Finesse," she said. She went to the bathroom, this time without the corkscrew in her steps. When she returned, she carried a cage with an animal jumping around it in frantic, maniacal twitches. A rat. A big, fat Los Angeles rat. The size of a goddamn rabbit.

"Finesse hasn't eaten in two days," she said. She set the cage right on my chest. The rat pecked at the peanut butter oozing up between the thin bars.

It tickled at first. Then I felt its tiny teeth scraping at my skin. I tried to scream. Her panties stifled my voice.

Patience put her hand on the latch to the front of the cage. "You two will have the place to yourselves for the next three days," she said. "Good luck." Then she opened it and rushed out of the room. She hung the "Do Not Disturb" sign as she shut the door.

I struggled for a while, whipping my body from left to right, throwing the rat, sometimes getting enough momentum to send it clear off the bed. It found its way back every time. My energy drained and I went into a daze. Maybe it was shock.

The rat chewed a hole into my belly while I stared at the walls. What I thought about at that moment was the times I'd stuck my gun in my mouth and practiced pulling the trigger. I always rationalized my ego's inability to let go as some sort of noble nonsense about "choosing to live." The *right decision*, as those chumps on daytime talk shows would no doubt have stated it.

"Patience" first appeared in *A Twist of Noir*.

KATY TOO

Heather's dad's friends showed up wearing ski masks. They both looked like rednecks, like Heather's dad. Wiry. Dangerous. Dirty jeans, plaid shirts, unbuttoned, and filthy T-shirts underneath. One of them handed her a dark, mustard-colored, stinky strip of cloth. "Wrap this around your eyes," he said. Katy sniffed it. It smelled like mildew and crotch.

"Do you have a clean one?"

"Nope."

Katy reached for her purse. The man who had given her the blindfold said, "Leave it. Got a cell phone on you?" She told him it was in the purse. "Good," he said.

She was scared, initially. The men led her outside to a car and helped her in. As the engine started, she forgot about her fear, worrying instead about the damage the blindfold might do to her hair. It was Saturday, which meant she'd washed it and used cream rinse to give it that extra bounce that made strangers look at her funny when she walked through the mall. She liked that, the way they looked at her. She was monogamous, however, and she had expected Billy Walker to be the same.

When she found out from her friend Lindsey, who heard it from Kylie, that Billy let his ex-girlfriend Cheryl give him a handjob in a booth near the back of Tubby's Pizza, on Thirty-eighth Street, she tore the head off of her Curious George stuffed monkey. She confronted Billy and he denied it at first. When he offered to break up with her, she told him that was unacceptable. Billy's dad was the CEO of Walker Investments. Katy had found her Prince Charming and she wasn't going to share him or his wallet with any other woman. She went to all her girl-friends at Ivy Tech for advice on how to make sure he never strayed again. Only Heather had an idea she thought would be effective. Her dad was some kind of thug from the south side of town. Katy didn't want to know too much. Criminals and stuff like that should only be on television.

Heather told her that her dad could teach Billy a lesson. "What kind of lesson?" Katy asked. Heather explained that she had been beaten and raped once by a bartender named Danny Box. Her father tracked him down and took him to a warehouse where some crazy guys smashed bricks into his dick until he couldn't walk. Katy said that sounded really "icky" and she wanted to have children with Billy. Breaking his penis wasn't an option. Heather assured her, "There are other ways to send him a message."

The girls met with her father. He was tall and skinny and stank like a bar, all whiskey and cigarettes. He dressed like a lumberjack and wore boots with steel toes. Not at all what Katy had expected, based on the few gangster movies she had seen when there was nothing else on television. His name was Walter, but he asked her to call him Pops. He said she was awful pretty and any boy dumb enough to cheat on her was probably queer. Katy said that wouldn't do. If Billy was gay, he was going to have to learn how to be normal. Pops laughed at that. "We can do some damage that'll scare him real nice." He told her five hundred dollars was the minimum. Katy asked why it was so expensive. Pops explained that he had to pay the men who would be doing the actual work. He started to tell her what was going to happen to Billy for that kind of money. She made him stop. "I want it to be a surprise." Then she asked, "Can I watch?"

Katy focused on the stench of the leather seats in the car, instead of the blindfold. She assumed she was in the back, by herself. The two men who picked her up were in the front. They were probably leering at her thighs. She had worn the highest, tightest black skirt she had, the one she was wearing the first night she allowed Billy to play with her breasts. When he tried running his hand between her legs, she slapped him. "I'm not that kind of girl," she said. She *was* that kind of girl, but she didn't want a rich boy thinking she was a whore. She made him wait two months before she even touched his pecker. He got so excited he messed up her white, denim skirt she bought at the GAP her senior year in high school. She was proud that it still fit her three years later. And the dummy just about ruined it with his baby-juice. She shifted her thoughts to the car she was in. Gangsters on television always drove big, luxury models. These were Southside Indi-anapolis shit-kickers, though. She decided it was either an ancient Lincoln or a Cadillac. Probably bought with dirty money. They showed stuff like that on Court TV. Then she heard the men talking about her.

"She's a piece of ass," one said.

"Hell, she's a *chunk* of ass," the other said.

A smacking sound, like one was giving the other a high-five. *Disgusting.* Men had a single-track mind. All of them. They didn't care about relevant things like shop-ping or television. "Where are we going?" she asked. She wanted them to talk about something other than whether or not she was a natural blonde.

"You don't need to know."

"Oh," she said.

The same man spoke. It sounded as if he had turned his head to face her. "Can I ask you a personal question?"

"Yes," she said. "I'm a natural blonde. *Duh.* Do you see any dark roots?" She tossed her hair around to prove it.

"Only one way to know for sure."

The other man said, "She looks like one of these mod-ern girls, you know? Shaves the puss so nobody knows what her real shade is."

Both of them laughed.

"That's not why I…" She shut up. They had managed to make a discussion of her hair-color sexual. Amazing. *They're like sharks.* She analyzed her frustration, something she sort of learned watching Dr. Phil and Jerry Springer. She wasn't really angry at the thugs. She was angry at Billy. This made her feel better about what was going to happen.

* * *

The car slowed down and veered to the right. Katy heard gravel crunching and shifting beneath the tires. They parked. The front doors opened and closed, then hers opened and she was helped out. The air reeked of decay. Smelled like a trash can with rotting meat in it. Maybe they were near a factory. Or possibly the animal burning plant near Greenwood. They led her by her elbows, one man on each side of her, across what she assumed was a parking lot. When they stopped, the man to her right let go. She could hear him struggle with a metal door, pushing it along a track that squealed as it rolled. She was nudged forward.

The door closed behind her. She smelled booze and cigarette smoke. Pops whispered in her ear, "Take the blindfold off and keep your mouth shut."

She did. As her eyes adjusted to the dim light, she saw that she was in a large, aluminum warehouse. Her drivers stood behind her.

Underneath a single, hanging bulb was a wooden table-chair. Seated in the chair was Billy. His hair was uncombed, a stupid habit he picked up watching celebrities on *TMZ*. He was in his Bears jersey, the one with holes all over it that Katy had begged him to throw out, and jeans she bought him to replace the pair he had been wearing since, she figured, puberty. His arms and legs were taped to the chair's arms and legs. He was gagged and squirming and trying to protest. He had on a blue blindfold. Katy wondered if it stank as bad as hers. Something developed in her stomach. She thought it might be a reaction to the teaspoon of humus she'd eaten for breakfast. Part of her wanted to laugh. Seeing Billy so helpless, she wanted to chastise him, ask him where his father was now, who was going to save him? More than that, she wanted to tell him exactly what he had done to end up there.

Standing on each side of the chair were two men who looked pretty much like the ones who had driven her there. With the exception of Pops, they all wore ski masks. Pops nodded to one of the men standing near Billy. The man walked off into the darkness. The creaking of wheels on a metal cart echoed across the warehouse, a handheld sledgehammer and a regular claw-toothed hammer on top of it. Pops motioned for her to follow him over to the cart. He pointed to each implement, the way a model on *The Price Is Right* might point to a fabulous new car or maybe an awesome set of jewelry. She understood what he was asking her. The unpleasant feeling in her stomach spread. She imagined a kitten, or maybe even a cute little puppy, in her belly, stretching its limbs. She took a deep breath. Pops pointed again, this time with jerky, impatient movements.

The sledgehammer looked too vicious. Pops pulled her back. The man on the other side of Billy walked around and picked up the claw-toothed hammer. He moved the cart out of the way. The pain in Katy's stomach felt like a hand, pulling down at her throat. She wanted to throw up, but her belly was empty. The man with the hammer turned it around and slammed the claw-end of it down on the center of Billy's left forearm.

The hammer landed with a thud and the claw cut into his skin. He tried to leap out of the chair but only succeeded in reinforcing the tape around his wrists and legs. His head shook back and forth. The screams forced through his gag came out in panicked wheezes.

The man with the hammer smashed the claw-side into the same spot until the thud was followed by a clicking sound that made Billy react so ferociously he brought the chair off the ground and turned it. Katy screamed and immediately grabbed her mouth. It was the most disgusting thing she had ever seen, with the possible exception of *Saw IV*, which her last boyfriend forced her to watch because he was a weirdo and that seemed interesting when she'd first met him.

Billy said her name through his spit-soaked gag— "Katy?" It was clear enough that everyone understood it and stared at her.

Pops sighed. He took the hammer from the man who had been using it. He brought it back to Katy and said, "You break the other arm."

She refused to take it. She was crying and couldn't speak without choking back her breathes. "I...don't..."

Pops grabbed her by her arm and shoved her toward the chair. He ripped the gag out of Billy's mouth and removed his blindfold. He wedged the hammer into Katy's hand. "Break his other arm. *Now.*"

She shook her head. She could *feel* Billy trying to make eye contact with her. She didn't want to see anybody, didn't want to *be* anywhere right then. "I can't," she said again.

"Katy," Billy said. "Please, Katy..."

Pops clenched his fist around Katy's hand holding the hammer and arched her over Billy's right arm. She tried to resist, tried to pull her body away. He drew her hand back and forced it to slam into Billy's arm, over and over, until the claw tore into the muscle and flesh and chipped the bone. He let go of her and she collapsed, sobbing.

Billy stopped moving. Katy thought he had gone into shock. She learned all about that on *ER*. And Billy said, "Don't worry, baby. My dad will get these guys."

Pops shook his head. He turned to the men Katy assumed had driven Billy there. "Eighty-six," he said.

They removed the tape holding Billy to the chair. One of the guys picked him up and draped him over his shoulder. The other man pulled Katy to her feet. They led them out of the warehouse, to the parking lot.

Her eyes adjusted once more. She was tossed into the back of a white, stretch van, along with Billy. He seemed to be in complete shock, carrying on about how he preferred blueberry Kool-Aid to strawberry Kool-Aid. Katy held her nose. The van smelled worse than the blindfold. There were dark red streaks along the walls. She felt sick again. As the van carried them away, she looked out the back windows. She had been wrong about the car that brought her there. It was an Oldsmobile.

"Katy Too" first appeared in *Beat to a Pulp*.

MY KIND OF TOWN

Jenna rested on Tom's chest. Both worked to catch their breath. Tom closed his eyes and allowed the different scents coming from his young lover to massage his senses. He grinned and realized, for the moment, just how happy he was.

"What are you smiling about?" Jenna bit his neck, then smacked his chest hard enough to snap his eyes open.

He brought her head up and kissed her. "Don't do that. I can get that at home."

She sighed, rolled off him. "Speaking of the devil," she said, "how soon?"

He looked out the only window in her bedroom. Past the smog from Gary and East Chicago, the setting sun bled orange over the Chicago skyline. "Even if I can get her to agree to the split," he said, "we'll still have to wait."

"Why?"

He assumed her inability to see the plan in a logical manner was a casualty of her youth. He didn't begrudge her. She'd had a tough life. Her mother was murdered by a serial killer from Illinois and her father died in an explosion at the tire factory he worked for in East Chicago. His generic life insurance left her just enough to maintain a small house on the edge of town. She was only twenty-two and she'd already lost her world.

"Let's say I file in the morning," he said. "How soon do you think it'd be proper to pack up and ship out?"

"Tomorrow night?"

"Believe me," he said, "ain't a thing I'd like more than to scoop you up and carry you off to fancy old Chicago. We got to be smart."

"Who cares what other people think?" she said.

"Maggie's sure to get a hell of a good lawyer to take a run at the stash," he said.

"The stash?"

"Stop playing dumb."

She frowned, brought her arms over her chest and pouted.

"I'm serious."

"I hate this town."

"Haggard ain't the problem," he said. "Life's mostly misery. Might even be true in Chicago."

Maggie was waiting for Tom when he got home. She was seated at the dinner table, one leg hoisted over the other, bobbing up and down.

He fixed himself a can of ravioli and took his seat on the opposite side.

"Is this the way it ends?" she said.

"What are you talking about?"

"You know damn well."

He took a drink of milk and sighed. "I'm the only one working at the station. How many times I got to tell you…"

Maggie stood, threw the crossword puzzle she was working on at him. "That dump ain't had any business since you bought it." Her face turned red.

"What's that got to do with anything?"

She walked around and smacked him in the back of his head. "Who are you sticking it to?"

He ignored her.

"Who the hell are you sticking it to!?" She hit him, over and over, with open palms.

He caught her hands and twisted them enough to stop her. He waited for her to calm down. "When was the last time you and I had us a close encounter of the tender kind?"

She said nothing.

"I can't remember either."

She picked her crossword puzzle up, sat back down, and tried to pretend the argument was over.

He finished his ravioli, stood and walked by Maggie to wash his dishes in the sink.

"Jesus," she said.

"What now?"

"You bastard." She put her head down on the table, slammed it a few times until he grabbed her by the hair and stopped her.

"Quit being so damn showy."

"I can smell that whore," she said. She repeated it,

again and again.

Tom let go of her hair and walked away. "I'm going to bed."

The alarm clock rang at six in the morning. Tom leaned over and hit the snooze button. His hand brushed across an envelope left on the top of the radio. He turned on the light on his side of the bed. Before opening the letter, he noticed that his wife was not next to him.

"Maggie!" He looked around, as though maybe she might emerge from thin air. He opened the letter and read it. "Oh Lord," he said. He picked up the phone next to the radio.

Sheriff Dale Hopper, probably hungover, spoke on the other end. "This better be good."

"Dale, I think Maggie's gone and done something stupid."

"Tom?" said the sheriff.

"That's right. Looks like she's killed herself."

"You sure?"

"Well, she wrote me a letter saying as much."

"She hang herself, or something?"

Tom realized he hadn't even looked around the house. He put his hand over the receiver and shouted. "Answer me, now, woman!" He went back to the phone:

"Ain't making a sound, wherever she is."

"Maybe she's moping somewhere in town."

"Could be."

"Let's not panic until we know exactly what she's up

to. I see her, I'll let you know."

"Thank you much, sheriff."

He walked into the living room and looked out the front window. The station wagon he'd given Maggie once he he'd bought himself a truck was not in the driveway.

"Well, shoot," he said. After deciding to let things reveal themselves on their own, he went about his normal routine of getting ready for a long day of doing nothing at his gas station.

Tom's father had been killed by one, or many, of the thousands of chemicals floating around Liberty Steel, a mill between Haggard and Gary. Something had gotten into his lungs and planted an unstoppable nugget of cancer. A civil action landed Ted Bolan a small fortune. He died and passed the money on to his only remaining family, his son Tom. Good thing, too.

Tom Bolan was a lousy student in high school. More interested in beer and girls, he was kicked out for failing classes. He spent some years in the military, fought in the original Gulf conflict, and came home just in time to see his father pass.

The war had made him paranoid and stupid, so he turned what remained of his father's fortune into cash and locked it in a safe in his house. Eventually he got bored and purchased a gas station hidden just off of I-65. The Shell right next to the exit ramp saw to it that his business never made a cent.

He spent his days watching a small black and white

TV set until five in the evening. Then, he usually went to Jenna's, took care of her, then home to hear his wife complain. His life had become a routine. Again.

He realized he wanted out of Haggard just as much as Jenna.

Halfway through one talk show or another, the phone rang.

Tom got into his truck and drove to the East Chicago River, near the southern edge of Haggard. As he pulled onto the bridge, he saw Maggie's station wagon, parked by the side. Dale Hopper's squad car was next to it.

The sheriff stared over the side of the bridge. Tom joined him, strained to figure out what he was looking at.

"That your wife's, or what?"

Shredded, white cloth swayed in the wind, caught on several branches of a tree jutting over the water.

"Lord," Tom said. He put his hand over his mouth. A dizzying rush of guilt passed through him. *I killed my wife...couldn't say no to a younger, prettier gal, my shallow, selfish...*He stopped, remembered the way things really were.

She started it. She was the one who didn't know how to be tender with another human being.

"Well?" Dale Hopper interrupted him.

He sighed. "We both know it's hers." He turned back around and walked over to Maggie's car. He put his hands on it, doing his best to remain composed. Calm. Rational.

"Going to need a statement from you." The sheriff worked on a lip full of chew as he spoke.

Tom looked at him as though he had just been stabbed. "You surely don't think…"

Dale put his hands up, waved off the thought. "'Course not, Tom. It's all about procedure, paperwork, you know. I'll need you to reiterate how you was at home and such."

They walked back to the side of the bridge. Tom looked at Haggard's drunken lawman. Even though they were the same age, Dale's face showed at least ten years more. Both had competed for the same girl in the twelfth grade, a homecoming queen named Lorraine. Once Tom was booted from Haggard High, Dale landed the girl and moved to Chicago with her. They were married for all of a year before a car hit Lorraine and killed her. He came back to Haggard, worked as deputy until Ron Quinn died and left the sheriff's job vacant.

Dale's marriage to Jack Daniels was sealed by that point. Word around town was that he generally passed out before the sun went down every single night. If he seemed cold and unsympathetic about Maggie, maybe he deserved to.

Tom said, "What next?"

"She left a letter, right?"

He nodded.

"We put her on the books as a suicide."

"You going to look for the body?"

Dale Hopper laughed. "This is Haggard, Indiana, not Chicago."

"So?"

The sheriff leaned back, away from the bridge. "Well, Tom, just how do you propose we go about looking for her body?"

"Don't you have a dog, a police dog, like on television?"

Dale shook his head.

"Ah, what's the stuff you use to swim underwater for a long time?"

"Scuba gear?" When Dale stopped laughing, he said, "Maggie's probably floating down the Chicago river right now, headed straight for Lake Michigan. If they pull her out, great, we go get her and put her in the ground here in Haggard."

Tom covered his mouth, the full weight of the situation sinking in with the sheriff's words. "And," he could barely speak, "what if she washes up here?"

"Same thing. Have old Bob Kulak take a look at her, pretty her up for the burial, then plant her at Pleasant Hill."

They looked back down at the white fabric.

"Dale," Tom said, "I can't say I feel a whole lot of sadness."

"Makes sense to me. You been complaining about your marriage for damn near five years."

"Should I feel guilty?"

"Over what?"

Tom couldn't figure out what he was supposed to feel.

Dale Hopper gave him a slap on his shoulder and walked to his squad car. He radioed for a tow truck for Maggie's car.

* * *

Around eight in the evening, Tom woke from a nap. He looked at the empty spot where Maggie had once slept. He had met Margaret Buell in the service. She was attractive but tough enough to hang with the guys. In Iraq, they watched the Bears on television together. She knew more about football than him. Funny, considering he'd played strong safety for the Haggard Steelers in high school. He came to consider her his best friend and they got married. Immediately, the tender moments all but vanished. She doled out sex once or twice a month, acted like even that was asking too much.

Eventually, he found Jenna Hunt. She was hurt, seeking a father figure, and Tom was still trying to win the beauty queen from high school he had lost to Dale Hopper and, ultimately, a drunk driver in Chicago.

A headache threatened the sides of his skull. He massaged his temples.

The phone rang.

"I heard the news." Jenna sounded like a child who'd just been told she would be spending the rest of her life in Disneyland.

"Yeah, it's terrible."

"It's great." She affected the voice everyone did when they were convinced Tom was a small child who needed to be lectured. "That woman has abused you, physically, emotionally, shoot, financially, for just about as long as I've been alive. She deserved unhappiness. You, the opposite. Now come over and see me so we can mourn her passing properly."

"We got to be careful."

"It's after dark. No one will see you."

He held his forehead with one hand. "I don't know…"

She shifted to a coy tone. "I'm cold."

"Trust me," he said, "nothing's creepier than being here all alone."

"Then get in your car and drive over."

"What if the sheriff's lurking around?"

"Dale hits the whiskey at six on the dot. If he ain't passed out yet, he's on his way."

"How do you know?"

She stuttered. She said, "'Because I was arrested my senior year and I spent the night in lock-up and I saw it with my own damn eyes."

Tom sighed. "Look, cookie…"

"Take the road behind the Wojowski farm," she said, "through the woods, no one will see you. I'm warming up right now. You don't get here within the next hour, I'll buy a machine and forget all about you."

She hung up.

"Damn women," Tom said. The last thing he wanted was to lose his wife and his girlfriend in the same day. He put on his pants, draped a button-down shirt over his shoulders, and headed out.

The stores were already closed. Even the Dairy Queen, the only national franchise in town. Nobody was on the streets. Tom considered whether it really was Maggie who was boring or just the place they lived. The more he thought about it, the happier he was that he would soon be in Chicago with Jenna. Taking a new stab at life, as it were.

He turned onto Seventh, the street running alongside Highway 65. The major and minor roads were separated by a clump of forest. Once he passed the Wojowski farm, the trees arched over the road. The only light came from his car. The stars above couldn't compete with the pollution spilling over from Gary and Chicago.

In the distance, he saw something standing in the middle of the road. Knocking the horn a few times, he assumed the object, probably an animal, would move by the time he got closer.

It was a person. A woman. A light shined on her from behind. She wore a white gown that flowed in the night wind.

And she refused to get out of the way.

He smashed his hand into the horn.

His foot inched over to the brake. Then he saw who it was:

Maggie.

He hit the brakes and turned the wheel at the same time. His car screeched around and spun three times into the forest before slamming into a tree. He blinked, made sure he was still conscious. His neck snapping around caused sharp stabs of pain all over his body.

The glass in the driver's side window had broken out. Maggie leaned in, careful not to scrape herself on any shards along the border. "You're hurt very bad," she said. "You need an ambulance."

He couldn't take his eyes off of Jenna, standing right behind her with a large flashlight.

"You didn't think I'd kill myself over you, did you?" Maggie said.

"I'm, I'm sorry." Jenna looked at her feet.

Maggie said, "Give me the combination to the safe. I'll send Jenna back to try it out. If you tell me the right numbers, she'll call me on my cell and I'll fetch you an ambulance."

He stared past her.

"Come on," Jenna said. "I don't want you to hurt anymore."

"Hush, girl." Maggie swatted her on her thigh. She leaned in closer to Tom. "Give me the numbers. All we want is the stash."

Jenna stepped forward. She had a small pad of paper and a pen in her hands. She held them out for Tom to see.

"Just get me to a hospital," Tom said. His breath came in quick rushes, as though he had climbed twelve flights of stairs.

"I can't do that." Maggie put her arm around Jenna's waist. "We're leaving this town. You can die here, alone, in the forest, or do as I tell you."

At that moment, Tom resented having been born an exceptionally stupid human being. Maggie had never been responsive in bed. She always made excuses for it.

"You have no choice."

It sounded as if one of the women had said it, though he was certain the voice came from his own mind. He gave them the numbers.

Jenna backed away. She refused to look at him.

"Go get it." Maggie snapped her fingers in her face.

Tom wanted to tell her to hurry up as well. He was under the impression they were speaking of the money he'd left in his safe.

"He's going to die anyway." Jenna looked as though she might break into tears.

"We can't take any risks," said Maggie. "Now, go get the stuff."

The stuff, Tom learned, consisted of two large canisters of gasoline and some matches.

The women doused his car and him. Then they lit him up.

Maggie kissed Jenna's forehead and led her away, into the darkness.

Maggie entered the house first. Jenna still held the combination in her hand. Tom had hidden the safe under the floorboards in the living room. Maggie knelt down and removed the planks of wood concealing it.

"I'm going to need some help getting this above ground," she said. She snapped her fingers at Jenna, then realized her young lover had let someone else in the house.

Sheriff Hopper stood behind Jenna with an arm around her shoulders.

"Whore," Maggie said.

The sheriff motioned for her to stand. "Let's go to the dining room and discuss business."

"You have no choice," Jenna said. "Sorry."

Hopper pulled out a chair at the end of the table, the one Tom normally occupied, and gestured for Maggie to sit.

"How long has this been going on?" she asked Jenna.

Before any further conversation between the women could take place, the sheriff produced a .22, forced it between Maggie's teeth, and pulled the trigger.

Jenna screamed and jumped back.

Dale wiped the gun clean and placed it in Maggie's right hand. "Now, let's see to that money."

They hoisted the safe onto the floor. Jenna wept. Dale grabbed her chin. He said, "Just what part of this did you think was going to be pleasant?"

"I know," she said.

"Now give me the numbers."

She didn't move.

Dale forced his hand into her pockets until he found the pad she had written them down on.

"What if Tom lied?"

"We'll crack this sonofabitch," said Dale. "One way or another."

The safe opened without any hassle.

Jenna's mouth dropped.

Hopper laughed, loud and hearty, shaking his head. "That idiot." He picked up the few bills remaining in the safe. No more than four or five thousand dollars.

"That idiot," he said again. "I knew his damn station was bleeding money, but, sweet Mother Mary..."

"You told me he landed a fortune from his daddy's lawsuit."

"He did, numbskull. And he sunk it all into that worthless gas station. Just to get away from his wife."

"That won't last us a month in Chicago." Jenna pointed at the money in his hand.

"Ain't nobody going to Chicago." He walked back into the dining room and took the gun from Maggie's hand. He pointed the .22 at Jenna and pulled the trigger. He shot her three times in the head and once in the heart. Her body collapsed, convulsed, then came still like a tire losing its last air.

He wiped down the gun once more and returned it to Maggie's hand. He put the money back in the safe and the safe back in the ground and covered it up.

"Looks like we're all stuck here," he said.

He drove to the police station to drink and sleep and wait for the dead bodies in Haggard to attract someone else's attention. Then he would be able to come along and do his job and nobody would be the wiser. "Can't get peace of mind like that anywhere else," he thought. "Not even in Chicago."

"My Kind of Town" first appeared in *Thuglit*.

A MATTER OF TIME

He followed him past the twenty-four hour tofu house at Kingsley and Wilshire. Inside the orange and green neon-coated temple, Koreans and yuppies from the west side slurped down healthy food served McDonald's-style. They laughed and howled between bites, unaware of any nastiness beyond the walls of the restaurant.

The man looked like he might be Salvadoran, or maybe from Chile. He had long, black hair, tied in a ponytail. He wore jeans and a jeans jacket. Enrique Paz wondered what he carried in the backpack slung over his shoulder. It was covered with buttons bearing political slogans. The guy was built like he could probably hold his own in a fair fight. He walked, in fact, like he prided himself on that very point. It didn't matter. Neither did it make a difference when he climbed the steps leading to the Our Lady of the Angels cathedral.

It was five o'clock. Cars and buses jammed the intersections. Proper people with proper jobs made their way out of the giant office buildings. Most of them walked with the stiff gait imposed by the standard uniforms of wage slavery: the men choked themselves with ties and the women were dressed in skirts wrapped around their waists so tight they looked like they might twist themselves into two. They hurried to the bus stop or parking lot or wherever their chariots were that took them away from the misery hiding on both sides of Wilshire.

Enrique was supposed to be meeting a couple of white boys from West Hollywood to sell them some meth. He had gotten to the internet cafe at Normandie and Wilshire ten minutes early. The place was packed, as usual. That was a good thing. It consisted of rows of cubicles people hid themselves in while they looked for their individual salvations on the World Wide Web. Enrique found a blue card in his wallet. Assumed he still had time on it. Sitting down at the first vacant system, he put the card in the reader to the right of the monitor. His face turned red as soon as the computer screen lit up. He hit the restart button, stood, and launched after the man who had been using it just before him.

"Yo," he said, "come here a minute."

But the man was out the door.

Enrique put his hand in his pocket. He curled his finger around the trigger of the gun he carried. Since he was dealing to white boys that day, he had only brought a .22. It would have been enough.

He followed the man into the cathedral. It was the same church his family held services in for his little brother, Herbert. Eight years old. They found his body in a green dumpster behind the McDonald's at Western and 9th.

The man who had killed Herbert had, according to his own confession, started the same way, looking at the same kinds of pictures on the internet. Enrique's father assured him the prisoners in San Quentin would realize proper justice. So far, they had not gotten any word on the pervert's demise. "It's just a matter of time," his father said, over and over.

Enrique splashed his forehead with holy water and crossed himself. "Forgive me, Father," he said. Afraid to look toward the ceiling, afraid God might crash through the brown stone, scoop him up right there and, with giant fingers, flick him straight to Hell, he kept his eyes on the ground until he got to the chapel.

Thin stained-glass windows allowed the high sun to paint the church with columns of light. There were a dozen people scattered throughout. They were all kneeling, praying. They were from everywhere. Latinos, white people, black people, and a lone Korean. High above the altar, a modern art, anorexic Jesus on the cross stared down at the flock with sinister judgment. It was carved out of wood.

Halfway to the front of the church, the man had slipped into a pew and was hunched over the bench in front of him. His eyes were clenched shut. Tears squeezed out and traced a river down the side of his unshaven face. His fingers were wrapped so tightly together they were turning white. He gently rocked his fists and forehead together and apart, together and apart, together and apart...

Enrique's chest began to heave. The plastic sheet of

conscience his parents and teachers and preachers had worked so hard to stretch across his common sense struggled to stop him. The voices he knew were not his own begged: *"It is a stranger. See the anguish in his face."*

"That means nothing," Enrique whispered. He sat down a yard away from the man. "Eh, amigo," he said. "You like pictures of little boys?"

The man's eyes were wide. He looked around. "What do you want?" He spoke in a quick, hushed voice, no doubt hoping no one else in the church would hear them.

"It doesn't stop," Enrique said. "Until you satisfy what the devil has planted in your heart, until you murder innocence. Nothing will save you."

Shaking his head, the man wept. "I can't help it."

"I know." Enrique pulled the .22 from his pocket and shot the man in the stomach. The pop from the gun bounced off the walls in one giant clap. It sounded as if someone had dropped a Bible on the stone floor.

Enrique waited for the crowd in the church to gather the courage to come closer and see what he had done. He had to contain his laughter as they gasped and screamed, then backed up, thinking maybe the crazy Mexican with the gun might shoot them next. He placed it on the pew to let them know his work in the church was finished.

"Somebody call nine-one-one," he said. *If there's a God, I'm on my way to San Quentin.*

"A Matter of Time" first appeared in *Powder Burn Flash.*

METHAMPHETAMINE AND A SHOTGUN

With Respect to Chester Himes

Debbie had been over earlier. She laid out a couple of rails. They topped off the crank with a joint she rolled in papers decorated like the American flag. After burning down Old Glory, they got busy on Ethan's bed. He only came once. It took him half an hour to get there, thanks to the dope. Debbie seemed happy enough. She put her clothes on and left without telling him where she was going.

Ethan sat up, his back propped against a cracked wall in his one room apartment. There was no kitchen. There were no windows that weren't holding broken glass together with tape and cardboard. Aside from the bed, there was only a folding table with two metal chairs by the door. That was where they had gotten high. Normally, Ethan would provide the drugs. His source had been buckled by the pigs. The only possession he had at this point was a Remington 12-gauge. A cop had traded it to him for some meth.

"We use these to take down fuckers on PCP," the johnny had said. "You shoot somebody nice and close, their head'll bust open like a hamster in a microwave."

Ethan was aware of everything relevant, which was *nothing*. Meth and heroin brought him to the same place, but in different ways. Smack allowed him to quietly accept mortality. Like an angel, gently rubbing his shoulders, whispering, "Someday you're going to die, and that's okay." Crank, on the other hand, made him feel as though possession of this knowledge hoisted him above common people who couldn't face the reality that their lives, at the end of the day, would mean nothing.

While he rode a wave of superiority, he felt the undertow of worry, rising from the depths of his mind, forming a hand, then a claw, wrapping its tough, leathery fingers around his skull. "I think I'm thirsty," he said. What he thought, however, was:

Why did Debbie leave so goddamn soon?

The claw grew larger and scooped him off the bed. The effort to move muscles and bones was easier than slicing through a lightly melted stick of butter. Walking across the room, he understood that his feet were heavier than the Earth. They bounced off the floor as though it were made of a million titties, waiting to nurse him if he chose to fall. He stopped at the table and looked at the shotgun. There were three shells next to it.

They met him on the elevator. Luckily, Ethan was alone. They started on his shins and elbows. He could feel their little feet scampering up and down and in circles. They were too cowardly to show themselves in the physical world. He was certain they were millipedes. When he started using meth he scratched them, opening his skin and marking himself an addict. Now he was wiser. They wanted him to tear himself apart. The enemy sent them. He tolerated the itching the way he put up with roaches and mice in his apartment.

In the lobby, the mailman stuffed clouds into thin metal boxes. Ethan bit his lower lip to keep from asking the guy just who the hell he thought he was, doing God's work without God's permission. Before he could get to the street, he broke out in laughter. "*I'm* God," he said.

The postman backed against the wall, his hands raised. "Anything you say, man."

Ethan pushed the glass doors leading outside open. He was still chuckling over his own mistaken identity. The palm trees lining both sides of the street waved to him.

Saturday afternoon in Koreatown. Children played on thin strips of grass between the apartment buildings and sidewalks. Their parents sat on steps talking. *Plotting.* "Your kids are smarter than you," he said. He pointed at the adults and every one of them jumped up and backwards. They ran to their sons and daughters.

"Don't even think about it!"

The adults stopped. They put their hands up. "Please," they said. They whimpered, cried, sobbed into the grass that danced to the same rhythm as the palm trees. They got on their knees and worshipped Ethan.

"That's more like it," he said. He headed up Ardmore, toward Third Street. There was a consumer temple on the corner of Kingsley and Third, just one block over. The way the sidewalk moved under Ethan's feet, he suspected the whole thing had been planned—his thirst, his paranoia about Debbie. *Why was she in such a hurry to leave?* When he turned onto Third, he saw the Kipling Hotel. A relic from the time before the world had been blessed by his presence. He crossed the street. Cars stopped for him. The people inside them pointed at him. Some grabbed their cell phones. Some made phone calls. Some even took pictures.

They know I'm God.

The front door to the Kipling swung open and a man in a suit and tie stepped out and put his hand in his pocket. Ethan wondered why anybody would be dressed like that on a Saturday. He watched the man pull out a set of keys and drop them on the ground. Then he saw *her*, sitting inside the SUV the man eventually unlocked and climbed into.

Debbie was in the passenger seat. She was in the back, as well. And sitting right next to her was Debbie. Even in the rear, where normal people put groceries and bowling balls, two more Debbies faced the opposite direction. In the driver's side, the man was trying to get the key into the ignition.

"You sonofabitch," Ethan said. He drew back and pointed a giant, angry finger at the windshield. The glass exploded into a star-shower of prisms. The interior of the car filled like a bath tub with red, boiling lava.

Somewhere, someone screamed, "Oh my God!"

Ethan nodded. Proud to be so easily recognized. He saw the harsh orange and green announcing the 7-Eleven across the street from the Kipling. The liquids in the money temple would wash away the snakes of worry burrowing permanent homes under his skin. He remembered root beer, a substance that worked on his temporary shell like gasoline in an engine.

"Debbie's there, too," he said. "I'm sure she is."

Cars screeched in the parking lot, peeling pavement like a banana skin, to get out of his way. Ethan put his free hand out and motioned for everyone to calm down. "Relax," he said, "you have my permission to exist." Two homeless guys opening the door for customers in hopes of getting spare change ran away as fast as they could.

Ethan laughed. "I hope you folks realize that kissing my ass won't help you. Not ultimately." He entered the convenience store.

The first thing he noticed was that Singh, the attendant on duty, was talking on the phone. He looked nervous. Ethan realized the short man, usually his friend, was hiding something. "Who's on the other end?" He pointed at Singh.

Singh dropped the phone and put his hands up.

Ethan could hear the voice coming from the receiver: "Sir? Sir?"

It was Debbie.

"You tagging my girl behind my back?"

"What?" Singh looked at the only other customer in the store.

It was a kid with a skateboard and Super-Gulp over-flowing with neon green bubbles. He held his arms out, pretending to be Jesus. "Mister, you're in big trouble," he said.

Ethan looked at the skater. "You fucking her too?"

"Who?"

"Debbie."

"No man. I ain't doing nobody named Debbie."

Ethan nodded. He stepped back. The kid dropped the cup and ran out the door.

Singh crept to the other side of the counter.

"Where do you think you're going?"

The clerk's white hair snaked around like it had been hooked up to electricity. The fluorescent lights bounced off his otherwise bald head in a basketball rhythm.

"Shame on you," Ethan said, his voice like a vicious thunderclap. His judgment was so severe the blood of the devil spilled all over the cigarette rack behind the counter. "I said I'd get to the bottom of this." He walked to the coolers and opened one of the doors. "I haven't been wrong so far." The rush of cold air made him think he had been reborn in an arctic region. He closed his eyes and saw himself on an iceberg, drifting over the ocean. The night sky in front of him bled blue into purple into black and stars pierced the curtain like the gaze of a million dead people, curious to see if he would put the last piece of the puzzle together.

Ethan opened his eyes, found a bottle of Barq's root beer, and walked back to the counter. He looked around for the cashier. "I'm a fair man," he said. He dropped two wrinkled dollar bills on the counter. They smelled like a farm he had visited with his mother when he was eight. Manure and pigs and horses and chickens, all rolled up together to manufacture a super-stench that never quite left his senses. Then he heard the sirens.

"I'm no fool," he said. The song shrieking through the air was anything but beautiful.

The front door opened and a skinny man in a dark uniform stepped inside. His hands shook. So did his voice. "Sir," he said.

Ethan realized the new customer was holding a pistol. A .40 caliber semi-automatic. The tiny finger pointed right at him. His face scrunched up. Ethan wondered if his eyes would collapse into his mouth. *The gall.* "You don't judge me," he said. Then he pointed right back at the johnny.

The officer jumped backwards through the glass windows protecting the store from the laughing wind. As shards spun in magic circles, Ethan saw a hole in the universe open up. A huge eye, all pupil and no color, stared back. *Even gods have fathers.*

He stepped over the cop, who was now wrapped in a sticky red blanket, and walked toward Ardmore. Crowds of people had gathered across Third Street, all of them looking as if they might run away, on command. Ethan smiled. More sirens scraped the summer blue off the atmosphere. They would have to come for him. He was going home to enjoy his root beer and the rest of his buzz. With all the competition out of the way, Debbie would no doubt return. If she was smart, she would apologize.

As he approached his apartment building on the corner of Fourth and Ardmore, he realized the sirens belonged to the police. Lots of them. The air filled from pocket to pocket with the annoying scream of emergency vehicles providing the illusion that something could be done to prevent the final tragedy. Ethan shook his head. He pitied everyone around him. "I'll help you," he said, "all of you." Then he remembered:

He was out of shells.

"Methamphetamine and a Shotgun" first appeared in *All Due Respect*.

LITTLE PEOPLE

September 13
10:31 p.m.

It took her forty minutes to find a pay phone. The city had gotten cheap, assumed everyone could afford a mobile unit and carried it with them wherever they went. She could have used hers, but then there would have been a record, something to tie her to the little man in the trunk of her car.

She found a gas station ten miles south on I-37, toward Bloomington. It was a local business. Merle's. The owner, maybe Merle or someone related to him, hadn't kept the place up. The giant, rotating metal sign with slanted, white letters had rusted and its neon arteries were busted. Sarah would have passed it had she not seen the yellow glow coming from the garage. She crossed the highway and pulled in. An attendant, a teenager, sat to the side of the lift in a chair, tilting it back with his foot propped against a table with a small television on it.

When she saw the old fashioned, half-sized phone

booth, just beyond the pumps, she turned the car off. She rummaged through her purse for change. Nothing. She scanned the floor and emptied the glove box. Nothing. "Dammit," she said. She got out and checked her skirt, hose, and blouse for blood stains. Satisfied she didn't look like someone who had hoisted a battered body into her trunk, she walked to the glass garage doors and tapped on one of the panes that wasn't broken.

The teenager glanced away from the television. From where she stood, Sarah could see the rims of his eyes were red. "Good," she said. The kid would most likely forget the whole exchange. Slowly, as though there were no such things as time and pressure and stress, the teen-ager moped over and lifted the garage door.

"Evening, ma'am." He smiled the way young men who haven't learned to conceal their primary thoughts often did. If the boy had been just a few years older, Sarah would have considered it smarmy. He was dressed in jeans, high-tops, and a T-shirt. No nametag.

"Hi there," said Sarah. "I need to use the pay phone. Could I possibly get change for a dollar?"

The boy scratched his forehead, harvesting layers of gray matter to find the appropriate response. "You got to purchase something. Gas, you know? Or maybe a candy bar. Otherwise I can't open the register."

"Seriously?" Sarah expected that kind of crap in the city. Halfway to the country, she figured, folks were sup-posed to be more decent. "I just need to use the phone."

The kid stepped aside. "Well hell," he said, "come on in and use ours. It ain't long distance, right?"

That wouldn't do. Anything less than the perfect excuse might lodge a useful memory in the boy's mind. "Yeah, it is long distance."

The teenager's smile curled into Sleaze City. "I suppose I could be convinced to let you make your call anyway."

Sarah refrained from sighing or laughing. Instead, she waved him off the way she might 'shoo' at a fly. "Forget it." She walked back to her car.

"If you decide otherwise," said the boy, "I'll be right here." There was so much hope in his voice. Sarah envied him. All the worries in his world consisted of getting high and getting laid.

As she walked around her silver Lexus, she stared at the trunk. Then she got an idea. She opened the back of the car. The little man hadn't bled much. Cleaning up after him wouldn't be as bad as she had initially calculated. His eyes were closed. He looked like any other animal would after being run over by a half-ton sedan. Sarah patted down his front pockets. She stuffed her hand in and pulled out four quarters. "Thank you, buddy," she said. She slammed the lid and stepped over to the pay phone.

She picked up the receiver to make sure it worked. The plate on the front instructed her to insert twenty-five cents. "The good old days," she whispered. She dropped a coin in the slot and dialed. "You better be home," she said. "Worthless pri—"

"Hello?"

"Daniel?"

"Who's this?"

She wanted to kill him. "It's Sarah."

"Oh, hey!"

She could hear him straightening himself out. She wondered, for a moment, if he was with another woman. That thought quickly evaporated. It was a relic from a time when she still cared about the personal lives of the men she slept with. "Are you busy?"

There was a pause. "Not at the moment."

"I'm in trouble. Big trouble."

"You're not pregnant, are you?"

She wished he had been there, right then, so that she could have smashed the receiver over his head. "I can't get pregnant. Dummy."

"Play nice," said Daniel. "I might find something better to do."

What a bastard. "Look, baby," she said, "I need your help. Real quiet, though."

"What time is it?"

"What does it matter?"

Silence. Uncomfortable. Finally, Daniel said, "Where are you?"

September 13
11:27 p.m.

Daniel Elbow had been watching the Bears on *Monday Night Football* when his boss Sarah called for a favor. She wouldn't reveal exactly what. He cussed at himself for most of the drive to Martinsville. When he became deputy prosecutor, he told himself not to get involved with the district attorney. It was impossible, though. Sarah Miles was powerful, intelligent, and sexy. She used everything she had to build a reputation as the toughest D.A. in Indiana. They worked together for ten, twelve, sometimes sixteen hours a day. No man and woman could spend that much time together and not, at the very least, get the urge.

Daniel was ambitious, more so, he believed, than even the almighty Sarah Miles. He wanted to be mayor. Then governor. Then senator. He had his navy suit and burgundy tie already picked out for the day he won the nomination for president from the Republican Party. He was put on this planet, he believed, to save America from the liberal virus he felt made it so difficult to prosecute criminals. Sarah Miles was his ticket. Getting on her good side would take him places. Part of that process, it turned out, involved relieving her stress after particularly brutal days at the city-county building. They met at motels in Plainfield or Avon and sweated out their frustration with marathon sessions in bed.

She told him to drive to the McDonald's just off of I-37. She had gotten herself in trouble before. Never anything too bad. But Daniel Elbow could not afford a scandal on Sarah's part. If she went down, he'd crash with her. Politics, nothing else.

When he arrived, he saw her Lexus parked near the trash dumpsters, in the dark. He pulled into a spot on the other side of the lot, got out, and hustled over to her. He noticed the front of her car had been smashed in. It looked like there was blood on the corner of the bumper.

Sarah rolled her window down. She was smoking a cigarette. She was supposed to have quit six months before. "Get in," she said.

He walked around to the passenger-side and did as he was told. Right away, he noticed her hands shaking more than usual. "What's going on?"

"I hit somebody. Killed him."

"Ah," he said, "you hit someone...And *ran*?"

She nodded. She looked like she might cry. She never cried. Even when the pressure of work made her walk hunched over, as though she were carrying the entire world on her back, she refused to show any signs of weakness.

"All right." he thought about it. "Nobody knows the law better than us."

"Never mind the goddamn law," she said. "I need you to help me dump the body."

He wiped his hand across his face. "Oh God."

"Never mind God," she said. "We're going to Brown County to throw the little guy into Lake Monroe. There's no debate involved." She put the car in gear and drove back to the highway.

It would take twenty minutes to get to the lake. Daniel wanted out of the situation, needed to think of a way to pin the crime on Sarah, where it belonged, without tarnishing his own reputation. He talked with her to distract her, to bring her around to turning herself in.

"Who is it?"

She lit another Camel. "How should I know? Some midget. I couldn't see him. I was driving on Meridian, south of the monument. I'm just driving along, you know, and wham! This little guy flies up onto my hood and rolls to the side."

"Why didn't you call the police? It was an accident, right?"

She flipped her hair over her shoulder and gave him her *I'm Sarah Miles, You're Nobody, Shut the Hell Up* look. "Of course it was an accident."

"So? You didn't have anything to hide."

"I panicked."

Daniel leaned away from her. "Were you, ah..." He tilted an invisible bottle.

"I told you I quit drinking last year."

"You also said you quit smoking."

"Look..." She pointed her cigarette at him, like a weapon. "Cut the third degree. I messed up, I know. I dragged the little guy around to the back of the car and put him into the trunk." She laughed. "You'd think he wouldn't weigh so much, being a midget and all."

"I believe they prefer to be called little people."

"What the hell does that matter? He's dead."

There was no way out. He had to protect Sarah for his own sake. "Anybody see you?"

"I doubt it. It was after rush hour. It was dark. Doesn't matter now."

* * *

They wound through the hills of Brown County and turned onto a gravel road leading to Lake Monroe. Sarah explained that she had purchased a chain and three padlocks at a Home Depot in Martinsville. She said she stole a cinderblock from the gas station she had called him from. "All you have to do is help me wrap him up and toss him into the drink." She pressed the button under the dashboard to release the trunk.

The back of the car rocked. Sarah whipped her head around. "Dammit."

Daniel heard two thumps on the ground. In his side-view mirror, he saw a tiny man stumble into the darkness.

"Get him," said Sarah.

Daniel jumped out and ran after him. He could hear the little man breathing and breaking twigs as he scrambled. Then there was silence. A tire iron swung from the darkness and slammed into his knee. "*Son of a...*" He buckled and tumbled into the dirt. He grabbed one of the man's legs and tripped him. Daniel rolled over. Bolts of pain charged up and down his body. He found the tire iron and swung blind. Cracked the little man's skull with one shot. "Hey," he said, poking the man. No movement. "Shit." He got to his feet and pulled the man by his shirt collar back to the car. The body was a lot heavier than he thought it would be.

Sarah helped him wrap the corpse in chains and attach it to the cinder block with the padlocks. They waded into the water with it. The air stank of fish. As soon as they could feel the bottom sinking away, they let go of the dead man. The lake wrapped itself around the corpse and dragged it under.

On the drive to an all-night self-service car wash in Bloomington, Sarah said, "I'm going to move for a dismissal of Tom Doyle's case."

This surprised Daniel worse than the tire iron had. "*What?*"

"Some of Tom's friends let me know why it wouldn't be a good idea to prosecute him."

"We've got murder one on him. We can put him away for good."

Sarah raised her blouse and turned her back to him. She made sure he got a good look at the brown and red arrow-shaped imprint in her skin, just under her bra strap. She described how it had felt, to be scorched with a clothes iron by Tom Doyle's gangsters. "The case is going to be dismissed. That's all you need to know."

Daniel stared out the windshield. The headlights opened up the road just in front of them. Not too far beyond, there was nothing but cold, country darkness.

September 13
6:07 p.m.

Sometimes Eugene still noticed how people gawked at him. He was thirty-five-years-old. He had been leered at his whole life. Even as a child, when his peers were roughly the same size as him. His head was larger than his body and that caused his classmates to notice he was different. Over time, he accepted that most people couldn't help but be fascinated by anything they deemed unusual. He assumed it was the same thing that compelled them to slow down and watch accidents on the side of the road. Essentially, they made themselves feel better, appreciating that they hadn't been born with the same condition.

And this late in life, it wasn't a condition at all. It was who he *was*. Eugene Cassell. Folks always asked him the same questions when they got the guts to sit down and talk with him—"Were your parents little people as well?" *No, my parents were oversized, like you.* "What do you prefer people call you, midget, or little person?" *Well, if you know me, call me Eugene. If you don't know me, why would you even be talking about me?*

Then the ha-ha-ha's. Almost anything he said was considered humorous. He could read a eulogy at a funeral and people would laugh. That, he could never figure out. Tall women gushed when they heard him speak. "You sound so manly," they told him. *Well, that's probably because I am a man.*

More laughter.

He gave up on trying to get along with the oversized world. He dated tall girls in college. They never considered him anything more than a novelty. Once he learned to accept himself, the so-called normal people became oddities to him. Every advantage they had they took for granted. Just when he was ready to settle into a life of loneliness, he met Brenda. She was a little bit shorter than him and had gone through the same stages of realization.

So while the condescending woman at the jewelry shop gushed and awed as he asked her to show him different engagement rings, he ignored her. The only thought on his mind was the look on Brenda's face. They were going to meet at Bucco De Beppo's, downtown, later. Nothing trivial, nothing stupid, like putting the ring in her spaghetti. Halfway through dinner, he would clear his throat, wipe his mouth with his cloth napkin. "Brenda,"—he rehearsed it over and over in his mind—"we both know life is a sick joke. That's what makes our relationship work. Our mutual allergy to manure." Then he would get down on his knees and take her hand. "I love you and I want you to be my wife and together we can go through life with our middle-fingers proudly aimed at the rest of the world. What do you say?"

Just about any other woman would find such a proposal offensive. Not Brenda. That's why she deserved to be married, to know that she was loved.

Eugene bought the finest platinum ring in the store. It cost him six months' salary, but he didn't care. Money was like just about everything else in life. It went away no matter how hard you tried to hold onto it. The woman who sold it to him said, without being prompted, "We can size it to her finger after you give it to her."

"Thanks." He let the assumption slide and put the box in his jacket pocket. Before leaving, he made change for the bus.

He rode the Metro east, to Meridian Street, where he would transfer to a northbound line. He stood by the bus stop kicking at pebbles on the sidewalk. He hummed his favorite song. Then he sang lyrics he had invented to go with it—"*Summertime, and the living's sleazy. Fish are humpin' and the girls are high...*"

He blacked out before fully comprehending the look in the eyes of a woman driving a silver Lexus that roared up onto the sidewalk and knocked him six feet backwards.

"Little People" first appeared in *All Due Respect.*

A MORAL MAJORITY

Nicole answered the door in beige Capri pants and a tight, black T-shirt. "Harold?" she said. "Ain't you early?"

The preacher had sweated through the coat of his fine brown suit.

Nicole stepped aside to let him in. "What's going on?"

"You have something to drink?" Harold paced the small, one room apartment. He stopped at the king-sized bed, looked at it funny, as though he had never been in it, then continued until he came back to the bed and stared at it once more. "Good grief, Nikki," he finally said. "This place is a mess."

She ignored him.

Harold noticed a full bottle of whiskey on one of two oak-stained dressers. "Are you going to offer me something to drink?"

"You see that fifth of Jack Daniels."

The preacher grabbed the bottle, spun the cap off, and drained half a pint from it. Whiskey ran down his chin. "She's done it," he said, then again, "she's done it, Nikki, she's done it."

Nicole leaned her back against the door. She pulled a

Lucky Strike from a pack she had rolled up in her sleeve. As she walked over to one of the dressers to find some matches, she said, "Who's done what, Harold?

"Connie Moore. Jesus Christ. She let herself get pregnant. Says it's mine."

"Wally Moore's daughter?"

Harold nodded.

Nicole's face twisted so much her mouth and her nose threatened to trade places. She found a box of matches and lit her cigarette. "She ain't but fourteen."

Harold stopped moving. "What does that have to do with anything?"

Nicole laughed. "I suppose them boys from the lodge who burn crosses out front is right. You Protestant folks is way superior to us Catholics."

Harold put the bottle back on the dresser and balled up his fists. "Nikki, I've got a situation and you're the only one in Haggard who'd know how to sweep it under the proverbial rug." He calmed down and opened his hands. "No offense."

Nicole rolled her eyes and spit when she exhaled. "None took, Pastor."

"So what's your thinking on this? What would you do, you know, if you got yourself pregnant from one of your clients?"

"I'd do what I always do. A doctor in Chicago'll reach in, grab that little monster, and yank it while it's still cooking."

"Good grief." The preacher scratched his head. "Are you talking about an abortion?"

"Pastor, please," said Nicole. "You going try and tell me you never had a girl scraped out?"

"It's not legal, Nikki. What would I say if my flock found out?"

"Well," she said, "you can sit around and wait for the girl to give birth normal-wise."

Connie Moore climbed out of her bedroom window and raced across the lawn in front of her family's tiny house on State Road 53. She wore her blue dress with big yellow roses on the shoulders, the same one she wore to church every Sunday.

She ran to Harold's Buick, ripped the passenger door open and jumped in. She leaned over and gave him a kiss on the cheek and squeezed his hand. "Thought I wouldn't ever see you again," she said. "I mean private like, like this, after what I told you."

The preacher pushed her away. "You weren't lying to me, were you?"

Connie shook her head. "Ain't bled in two months."

"Okay," Harold said. "We'll take care of that problem tonight."

Connie looked confused.

"We're going to Chicago. There's a doctor there who will deliver the baby ahead of schedule."

Connie's lower lip shook. "Chicago?" she said. Harold suggested she find something to listen to on the radio. She tuned it to a station out of West Lafayette playing music he assumed had been recorded by the devil. He asked her who the noisy singer was and she told him, "Pat Boone."

"Let's try something else," he said. He pushed the dial to a gospel channel broadcasting from Crown Point. Hank Williams sang "When God Came and Gathered His Jewels." Harold smiled.

Connie looked out her window. She twirled her dusty-blonde hair with one hand and pulled at her bubble gum with the other. Once, she actually told Harold she wanted to be an astronaut. It seemed crazy to him that she would entertain such a thought, even as a joke. He glanced over at her and saw tears crawling down her face. "What are you sniffling about?"

She wiped her nose with the back of her hand. "I thought God was showing me how much you loved me. Like He showed Mary."

"Mary was a virgin."

"So was I."

"Look, I'm not God. You're not Mary."

She cried.

The preacher put his right arm around her. "You've got your whole life ahead of you. You're going to meet a nice, young man someday and he'll make you honest and you'll forget all about our time."

The girl buried her nose into the side of his shirt. He patted her gently, like a small animal.

They passed Gary and East Chicago. The radio drifted into static. They cruised up the Dan Ryan Expressway. Harold turned off on Thirty-fifth Street and idled near Comiskey Park. He looked at the piece of paper with directions to the doctor Nicole had recommended. As he studied them, Connie sat up.

"Baby's making my boobs bigger," she said. She peaked down the top of her dress.

The preacher followed her gaze. "I see that, sweetheart." He put the instructions away and pulled into traffic. "We're almost there, now."

They wove through neighborhoods that folks in Indiana would describe as "bad." The houses had broken windows repaired with pieces of cardboard. The grass in the gardens out front grew as tall as the rusted fences surrounding them. Music coming from passing cars sounded foreign to Harold. Worse than even Pat Boone. While sitting at a stoplight, he asked Connie if she recognized the singer blasting from a polished Cadillac next to them.

"Sam Cooke," she said.

He turned onto Michigan Avenue and found the building. Parked across the street. The doctor's office lurked at the top of a three-story building. Nicole told him to have Connie climb the wooden steps on the side facing the alley. He pulled an envelope stuffed with cash from the collection box out of his coat pocket. After explaining to her where to go, he handed her the money. "Knock twice," he said. "When the doctor answers the door, ask him what seven times seven is."

"That's simple," said Connie. "Forty-nine."

The preacher kept his cool. "Sweetheart," he said, "it's the password. It's how he knows you're not the police."

Connie got out of the car. Her shoulders jerked up and down as she walked. Harold assumed she was crying again. He felt bad for her. *I can't have any bastard babies,* he remembered. To distract himself from his conscience, he tuned the radio, looking for another gospel station.

A commotion coming from across the street woke Harold up. An orange AMC Rebel pulled into the alley. A woman in a skirt and a thick sweater got out and ran up the stairs at the front of the building. When she reached the top, a man waiting there loaded her arms with two huge cardboard boxes. He shooed at her and she bounced back down and put the boxes on the ground while she opened the gate on the station wagon.

The man from the top of the steps produced two more boxes from inside the office and hustled to the car without even shutting the door. Harold wondered if that was the doctor. Then he wondered about Connie. The man got into the station wagon. The woman nearly tore the pavement up as she peeled out.

All went quiet save Bill Monroe on the radio. Harold waited for Connie to show up. The office remained dark. He finally said, "That's odd." He killed the engine and got out.

The preacher climbed the staircase. Rotting wood creaked under his weight. He held tight to the railing. He got to the top and reached for the door. Then he stopped himself, thinking that touching anything would be a bad idea. He slipped inside the office and saw that it was just a small apartment with a kitchen and bathroom near the back. Aside from a table and three metal carts, the place was empty.

Connie lay on the table, her upper-half covered with a blanket, her legs and midsection bare. A streetlamp just beyond the window provided enough light for Harold to make out a pile of bloody fragments taken, he assumed, from inside of her, dripping down the edge of the table to the floor. Her thighs were soaked in blood.

"Connie?" he whispered.

He walked to the other end of the table, wrapped his sleeve over his hand and removed the white sheet hiding the girl's face. Her eyes were frozen open.

"Good grief," he said.

Once on I-65, back in Indiana, he allowed himself to feel bad for her. She had been nothing more than a pretty girl who sat near the front in church and had introduced herself at an Easter mixer the year before.

Harold Hornung conducted the funeral service for Connie Moore. The doctor who killed her had been caught in St. Louis, trying to get to Mexico. He told police the girl had shown up all by herself.

The preacher read a sermon prepared by his wife:

"I can't explain what this world is coming to; while our young men sacrifice themselves in Vietnam for the freedoms that make this country the greatest on the Earth, their peers at home sit down in streets and universities, frying their brains with the devil's weed, claiming they know better than the president of the United States what is and is not moral."

He wiped sweat from his forehead.

"I can tell you what's moral, brothers and sisters. Preserving the sanctity of life, both the lives of those who walk the Earth on their own and those carried in the wombs of God's most delicate creation, woman. And when a woman denies that sanctity to herself and to the seed growing inside her, I do believe we have reached the saddest stage in the human adventure."

Wally Moore and his wife Elizabeth stared at him with twisted faces.

He ignored them.

"Connie Moore was possessed, at some point, to engage in activities reserved for a grown man and woman united in the bonds of matrimony." He looked at a group of fourteen-year-old boys, classmates of Connie's. "I don't know who it was that planted the seed in her," he said, "but what I do know is that she felt the father was not worthy of seeing his own child open its precious eyes. While I'm sure Connie will be forgiven by our Lord and Savior, Jesus Christ, I'm also sure she will be spending eternity with her child in heaven where, I pray, she can explain to the poor soul why she chose to engage in such a brutal act of matricide."

The Wednesday after Connie's funeral, Harold paid his weekly visit to Nicole O'Brien. When she opened the door for him, she scowled. He asked her what her problem was. "Nothing," she said. She walked to the bed, pulling her skirt down along the way.

"We're not going to talk a little?"

She slapped her left butt cheek and said, "Let's go, preacher."

He stepped in and closed the door. "Don't you want to finish your cigarette?"

She laughed. "You got two seconds to get your tiny pecker over here."

Harold unzipped his pants and moved into position behind her. Nothing happened. "Good grief, Nikki," he said. "You've got me distracted." He closed his pants and sat on the bed.

Nicole pulled her skirt up and plopped down in a wooden chair by the only window in the room. She smoked her cigarette and glanced out at the concrete mixing plant across the street. "Klan torched another cross on the lawn tonight."

"I noticed."

"This country ain't ever going to accept us, is it?"

The pastor asked her what she meant.

"Catholics. Me. Hell, anybody who ain't Protestant and willing to lie straight through his teeth."

Harold laughed. "Well, Nikki, truth be told, this really isn't your country. We tolerate you, and when we don't need the entertainment you provide, we send you back home or lay you down with the worms."

"But the kids today, they're going to change all that."

Harold Hornung smiled. "Won't take us ten years to turn things back the way they're supposed to be. I promise you."

"A Moral Majority" first appeared in *Paraphernalia Quarterly*.

THE RALPHS AT THIRD AND VERMONT

The Riots

You remember when the Ralphs on Third and Vermont stretched across the entire block? Before the riots. Before those motherfuckers brought shit north, past Wilshire Boulevard. Set the best parts of the city on fire. No cops, baby. Too busy protecting Hollywood, Beverly Hills, Malibu. Like those motherfuckers from South Central had time to go that far west. *Shit.*

By the third day, everybody got in on it. Only people who gave a damn about their stores were the Koreans. Unlike the dumbfucks in Simi Valley, they'd been paying attention. The Koreans had guns. Patrolled their roofs, their parking lots, shot at anybody who looked like they needed it. Lucky for us, they were the only shop owners with the guts to stick around. Here's what I got when that shit went down:

1. A used toaster from the kitchen of the Jack in the Box on Vermont (pawned it at a joint on Hollywood

Boulevard a few months later).

2. A brand new shopping cart from the Vons on Third.

3. A sturdy thermos from the drug store on Oxford (lost it on the twenty line going to Santa Monica).

4. A case, motherfucker, a *case* of Bud and three bottles of Cisco (remember that shit?) from the 7-Eleven on Kingsley.

5. A small reclining chair I took from someone's apartment while they were off snatching some free shit for themselves.

I pushed that chair around on the cart until it became a nuisance. Then I dumped it on a bonfire burning right smack in the middle of Western and Third. Sat in the cart drinking the rest of the beer, which had gotten pretty damn warm by that point, watching those flames snap, crackle, and pop. The old fucks who stand outside the 7-Eleven, holding the door for Koreans and Mexicans, gave a ton of shit to Charlie—*You better hide yourself somewhere, white boy*! And Charlie, he stared at that blaze like he was hypnotized. Said it reminded him of some poor motherfucker in Bangkok.

"Just lit himself on fire," he said.

I said, "Buddhist, or something?"

He said, "No. Just a father, pissed off his daughters were giving it to American soldiers for cigarettes instead of cash."

"Damn," I said.

"Yeah," said Charlie.

I asked if he ever fucked any of those Thai girls while

136

he was there.

"Nope," he said. "Plenty of pussy in Saigon."

"Damn," I said.

"Yeah," he said.

The fire on Western spread, same as the riots. Spread across Third to Vermont. Long way. Crept into the parking lot of the Ralphs and, after motherfuckers tore out the side of the building, that fire walked right in and turned those empty shelves into modern art.

Charlie

Everybody called him Charlie because of his long stringy white hair, full beard and mustache. Wore jeans and a jeans jacket so ratty they looked like they had been dipped in oil and dried in the sun. Only thing he didn't have was that goddamn swastika on his forehead. So yeah, we called him Charlie. He said he came back from Vietnam with the spike. Couldn't shake it until he married the bottle. Said that never *really* did the trick. "Ain't got money for junk," he'd said. "I guess Boone's got to do until the Good Lord takes mercy and cuts me down for good."

Myself, I got better with age, even living on the damn streets. Sun did me right. Rich girls from west of La Brea, they still jock me for a thrill fuck. You ever lived on the streets, you know what I'm talking about. Poor Charlie, he dried like a prune, looked like a corpse before he turned fifty. Frail, nasty. Those white girls in nice cars stopped giving him charity just before the century flipped.

But everybody in Koreatown—Koreans, Mexicans, and the few white people left—they all knew and loved Charlie. Ralphs should have hired him. He stood by the door and offered to carry groceries. People would pay him ten, sometimes twenty-five cents per bag. That man never went to sleep without a bottle, let me tell you.

It was in the fall of 2004 when some boys from USC took care of Charlie. Those days, folks from other neighborhoods shopped at the Ralphs on Third and Vermont for one of two reasons—the first was the fact that the Mexican girls working the registers didn't give a shit about the drinking age. USC brats were always buying beer there. More refined people, they stopped in because word spread across Los Angeles that the deli cook, Leticia, broiled the best damn chicken in the known universe. Four wings and thighs for five bucks. No lie, baby. I don't care how good you think your mom or dad grilled a bird, this woman knew what she was doing. For most of us living on the street, we'd save for a bag on Thanksgiving or Christmas. Put away dimes and nickels for months, walk in, smell that chicken from the other side of the store, hopefully have enough for some beer to go with it (or the energy to steal some from the 7-Eleven). We'd sit in our spots, mine being a bench behind Our Lady of the Angels on Kingsley, and eat that shit like it was the finest pussy on the planet. Charlie loved that chicken, too. And he got it more often. Regulars at Ralphs would ask him if he was hungry, knowing damn well the answer.

"Chicken sure would sit nice on my belly," he'd say.

Even Koreans will buy a man a bite to eat if they know that's *exactly* what their money's going to. Charlie would help someone carry groceries and, just before they took off, after giving him some nickels and dimes, they'd smile and pull out a white, smoking bag of Leticia's legs and wings. He bowed, regardless of who gave him the food.

"Thank you very much," he'd say. He sounded like Elvis and he knew it. Worked it. Especially on the ladies, back when he didn't look like a Muppet. He once told me he'd come from a religious family. Alabama. Maybe Mississippi. Around here, nobody knows the difference and nobody cares.

When there was no action, Charlie took a broom the manager had set by the door and swept the walk. That motherfucker swept *without being asked*, without being *paid*. Said to me, "You don't expect me to work in a pigsty, now do you?"

Well, a trio of white boys from USC pulled in to the Ralphs. Cream-colored SUV. Looked like a Caddie. They let the rest of us know they had money and we didn't, walking around in their goddamn checkered boxers, their goddamn golf shirts, the kind my friends and I made fun of in the eighties. Their Trojan ball caps were turned sideways and backwards, like those goofy motherfuckers were gangbangers from Crenshaw or something. Stupid-ass plastic sunglasses over their eyes. And they brought their little white girlfriends with them. Short shorts, so damn short their ass cheeks spilled out the bottom, the kind of shit you could only see in porno movies when I was coming up. Tight, tank-top T-shirts, Greek letters inflated like balloons across their plastic titties.

Charlie stood by the south door. I worked the north with a crazy fuck named Wendell. Wendell used to blow a broken trumpet, same three notes, all over Koreatown. Folks gave him money, I suspect, just to shut him the hell up. Watched him get thrown off his spot by the Hollywood Video three times in the same night once.

Charlie nodded to the USC kids, said "How do you do," which he said to everybody.

One of the boys, let's call him Moe, pushed him back, said, "The fuck you looking at, *loser?*"

"Come on," said the girl closest to him. "He can't help it."

Another boy, Larry, if you like, said, "He needs to get a fucking job."

And the last one—might as well be Curley—said, "Fucking parasite."

Their women disengaged, gave them looks like, *You all don't pretend to have a goddamn soul, you can forget about getting any pussy tonight.*

I balled my hands into fists, imagined throwing those filthy motherfuckers through one of the plate glass windows. Wendell said, "You know them boys' daddies got a different lawyer in every pocket."

I said, "How much of nothing they going to take from me?" I moved sideways, like I wasn't paying attention. Snagged my pants on a table of rotting oranges. "Shit," I said. Took a second too long to free myself.

The college boys insisted the girls go into the store.

Then Larry and Curly shoved Charlie hard enough to send him over the rail by the door. The little fuckers laughed. One of them actually called him a *"douche,"* with that stupid-ass emphasis on the *d*.

Charlie's legs were caught on the rail. Maybe he'd gotten buzzed already, couldn't figure out the difference between the sky and the concrete. I heard him cussing. Hustled over and helped him to his feet. "What you putting up with that shit for?" I said.

He brushed the back of his jacket. "They're just funnin'," he said.

"Bullshit," I said. "Their daddies forgot to smack them for shitting their diapers. Somebody needs to fix that slack, know what I'm saying?"

"You slap those kids around," he said, "they'll just call the cops. You know how this story goes."

"Fuck that shit." I charged into the store. Ranchero played on the stereo. The scent of Leticia's chicken called like a damn siren. Most folks minded their own, pushing carts, grabbing cereal and whatever else. I spotted the SC kids in the booze section. "Yo," I said, walking toward them. Their women scattered, like they'd seen a herd of bison.

Moe said, "What you need, homeslice?"

Homeslice...motherfucker.

They huffed their chests, let me know they were real proud of the hours they spent shooting steroids and lifting weights.

"You best scoot your ass outside and apologize to Charlie," I said.

"Who the fuck is Charlie?" said Curley.

"You know who I'm talking about."

Larry tried to push me away. I spun him and shoved him into a stack of cases. He stopped himself, stopped the beer from collapsing on his head. His friends made a move, one from each direction. Moe swung first. Slow as fuck. I ducked, let him graze Curley's nose. They got mad at each other, spewed the only other insults frat boys have ever known:

"*Faggot.*"

"*Pussy.*"

The manager rushed over. Gustav. Skinny Salvadoran with glasses. Fought in the revolution. Let me use the toilet in the mornings. He machine-gunned some Spanish at us, then realized we didn't understand. "What is this," he said, "all of you." He gave me a fatherly kind of look, like, "*You* know better."

Larry sulked, like he was working on an Oscar. "This guy just came in here," he said. "He just started picking on us for no reason."

Rich folks always considered the rest of us idiots.

"This man," Gustav said, pointing his chin at me, "this man does nothing for no reason." He glanced at the college girls.

They shrugged, tilted their heads at Larry, Curley, and Moe.

Moe said, "Why would we lie? We're just here to get beer for the game."

"Go Trojans," said one of the girls, like anybody in Koreatown gave a shit.

"All of you," said Gustav, "take your problem somewhere else." He leaned toward me and said, "No bathroom for you, not for a week."

Curley slammed his fist into his other hand. "We don't get any beer, Holmes..." He punched his palm a few more times.

"Let's go," said Moe. He sounded convinced he had the high road.

I kept right behind them. Made sure they passed Charlie without giving him any extra shit. We watched them climb into their SUV and drive away. Figured that would be it.

To this day, the old motherfuckers outside the 7-Eleven insist it's not my fault what happened. But I could have done something. I could have figured out what kind of car those boys were driving. Could have gotten some idea what the license plate number was. Instead, I told Wendell, "So long," and headed to my afternoon spot near the depot on Wilshire and Vermont. The ESL teachers would be going home right around then. They were always good for a handful of nickels and dimes.

Later, I cruised to Oxford, floated between Denny's and the Hollywood Video. Put together enough coins to buy a bottle of Wild Irish, a pack of Kools, and some Twinkies for the night. A breeze shot down Western as I made my way to Third. I wanted to rap with the old folks at the 7-Eleven before settling behind the church.

In the distance, Charlie hustled around the corner

clutching a bottle and a bag of chicken. He booked into an alley behind a barbecue joint. A cream-colored SUV roared across the lanes, followed him. I said, "Shit," stuffed my Twinkies and smokes into my pants, and took off running. Then I heard screams. Women, shouting in Korean. Orange light danced from the alley. Got bigger and bigger, like a monster in a Bugs Bunny cartoon. Koreans filled the parking lot with their cell phones raised, like weapons. They looked confused and terrified. Then I heard Charlie, howling for his life.

The SUV screeched from the alley, raced past me. The little shits from SC tossed an empty gas can at me. "Suck on this," said Larry, or Moe, I wasn't sure. He was close enough I could have reached out, grabbed the motherfucker, pulled him from the car, and stomped him into the pavement. Wouldn't have lost a moment of sleep if I had. But they were gone, racing up Western. I thought I saw them turn on Melrose.

When I made it around the corner, a couple of young Korean cats were throwing newspapers on Charlie. I'd never seen anything like it. He'd become a shadow, wearing fire like a suit. He wouldn't stand still.

"Charlie!" I said. "Drop, motherfucker, drop!" My vision blurred from the heat.

He ping-ponged off of walls and garage doors, hollering, "Lord, help me!"

I grabbed one of the Korean girls who'd been waving her cell phone like a tennis racket. "Nine-one-one, now!" I said.

She looked like she had been slapped.

144

"Please," I said, my voice cracking, "call nine-one-one."

She nodded. "Yes, yes," she said.

Charlie must have been exhausted. He finally collapsed. His body shook, as though he were *cold*. As soon as the Korean girl finished her call, I heard the sirens. Not nearly close enough to make a difference.

Cops showed first. Talked to me for about five minutes. I told them to go to the Ralphs on Third and Vermont. "People saw them," I said, "ask Gustav. He's probably got a better memory than me."

They asked me to describe the SC boys. I didn't know what to say. The lone white cop grunted, actually said, "Oh, so we all look alike?"

How I wanted to put my foot in his ass right there. I calmed myself and described Moe. I said, "And, yeah, the other two looked the same. *Exactly* the same."

"You're just full of stereotypes," said the white cop.

Stereotype...unbelievable. I'd have bet my Kools and my Twinkies that was the biggest word that cop knew. Probably heard it on a talk show. I felt like calling him a dumb piece of shit, since no one else had ever done him the courtesy.

But I still remembered what those motherfuckers did to Rodney King.

And all this went down while Charlie convulsed and died. When the smoke cleared, there was nothing but charred meat and black gravel. Like he had never been a human being.

After the Riots

You could make the argument that Koreatown didn't ever recover from the riots. But things got back to normal after a few months, you know, mostly. I remember in the fall of '93, Charlie, Wendell, and me were picked up by three chicks in a BMW. Two of them were actresses, said they'd just shot a movie about ass-kicking cowgirls. The other one was a weather girl named Jill. Smoking hot. They said they wanted to get dirty. Rich girls always said that. They said, "We've never done anything like this." Rich girls always said that, too.

We didn't give a shit. Women out for a thrill fuck were good for sex, booze, and food. Sometimes they had blow, too. In those days, when the women still paid attention to Charlie, I had to watch out, make sure he didn't get down with some girl who'd turn him right back on to the dangerous shit. That night, though, everything was sweet.

The ladies drove us to a beach house in Malibu. Jill, the weather girl, said it belonged to her benefactor. Charlie fucked up, said, "You mean your Sugar Daddy?" I thought they'd eighty-six us, make us walk back to Koreatown.

She said, "Don't be offensive," and shrugged, like she hadn't been offended in the first place.

The house had big, gorgeous windows looking out on the Pacific. The waves rolled onto the beach so steady, made me think of time, made me think nothing would ever really change. We went into separate rooms, per the ladies' choices, gave them what they wanted, then spent the night drinking beer, sitting on a giant, u-shaped couch, in front of a fireplace, just talking. Wendell spun a heap of bullshit about playing horn with John Coltrane, back in the day. All that effort, then one of the actresses said, "Who's John Cold-train?"

The women said they wanted to know how we ended up homeless. Charlie got around to rapping about Vietnam. Spoke about the Vietnamese women, the dope, and how he knew he had been afraid all the time he was there, but couldn't remember how that actually *felt*.

"You were in a war?" said the weather girl.

"Yeah." He looked down. He always did when he talked about the war, like he had done something so terrible, even the Padre at Our Lady of the Angels would never forgive him.

"Did you kill anybody?" said one of the actresses.

"I don't know," he said.

The weather girl said, "Hope you didn't. Because, you know, *karma*."

Charlie sneered. "Do you even know what that word means?"

"*Duh*," she said. Then she stood and said, "Who needs another beer?"

"The Ralphs at Third and Vermont" first appeared in *Beat to a Pulp*.

Alec Cizak is a writer and filmmaker from Indiana. His work has appeared in several journals and anthologies. He is the author of three novellas, *Down on the Street*, *Between Juarez and El Paso*, and *Manifesto Destination*. He is also the chief editor of the fiction digest *Pulp Modern*.

nomoralcenter.blogspot.com/

On the following pages are a few
more great titles from the
Down & Out Books publishing family.

For a complete list of books and to
sign up for our newsletter,
go to DownAndOutBooks.com.

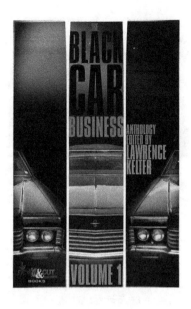

The Black Car Business Volume 1
Lawrence Kelter, Editor

Down & Out Books
April 2018
978-1-946502-53-7

It's the sedan just within sight that seems to be mimicking your speed and movements as you walk down the dark deserted street late at night. As the hairs rise on the back of your neck you wonder, who is behind the wheel and what is the driver's intent? It's The Black Car Business and its presence means your life is about to abruptly change.

Contributors: Eric Beetner, J. Carson Black, Cheryl Bradshaw, Diane Capri, Jeffery Hess, Lawrence Kelter, Dana King, Allan Leverone, Simon Wood, and Vincent Zandri.

A Scholar of Pain
Grant Jerkins

ABC Group Documentation
an imprint of Down & Out Books
February 2018
978-1-946502-15-5

In his debut short fiction collection, Grant Jerkins remains—as the *Washington Post* put it—"Determined to peer into the darkness and tell us exactly what he sees." Here, the depth of that darkness is on evident, oftentimes poetic, display. Read all sixteen of these deviant diversions. Peer into the darkness.

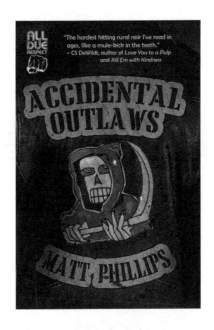

Accidental Outlaws
Matt Phillips

All Due Respect,
an imprint of Down & Out Books
978-1-946502-44-5

Three linked crime novellas that follow working class antiheroes as they indulge in theft, murder, and lawless shenanigans. Ain't no cops running things out this way. In "Mesa Boys," Ronnie plots a haphazard heist with a twisted con man. In "The Feud," tough-as-nails Rex lets his resentment for a local pot dealer cloud his judgement. And, in "Bar Burning," a mysterious drifter goes toe-to-toe with his new lady's psychotic ex-husband.

hurt hawks

MIKE MINER

Hurt Hawks
Mike Miner

Shotgun Honey, an imprint of
Down & Out Books
978-1-943402-72-4

When Patrick Donovan learns that Chris Rogers, a soldier who rescued him and took a bullet in his spine in the process, has been murdered by local thugs, guilt nags him. He and his men will tear Dorchester, Massachusetts apart to find the gangster responsible and avenge Chris's death. But nothing in life is simple. When Chris' young son takes matters into his own hands, the stakes are raised and Donovan faces a choice. Walk away or sacrifice himself for Chris' wife and child.

Donovan is done with walking away.

D

CPSIA information can be obtained
at www.ICGtesting.com
Printed in the USA
LVHW04s1618010518
575556LV00003B/597/P

9 781946 502971